The Twilight of the Golds

a play in two acts

by

Jonathan Tolins

SAMUEL FRENCH, INC.
45 WEST 25TH STREET   NEW YORK 10010
7623 SUNSET BOULEVARD HOLLYWOOD 90046
LONDON   TORONTO

For Mark

THE TWILIGHT OF THE GOLDS by Jonathan Tolins was presented by Charles H. Duggan, Michael Leavitt, Fox Theatricals, Libby Adler Mages, Drew Dennett, and Ted Snowdon at The Booth Theatre, New York City, on October 21, 1993, with the folowing cast:

DAVID GOLD .... Raphael Sbarge
SUZANNE GOLD-STEIN .... Jennifer Grey
ROB STEIN.. Michael Spound
PHYLLIS GOLD .... Judith Scarpone
WALTER GOLD .... David Groh

THE TWILIGHT OF THE GOLDS was directed by Arvin Brown. The sets were by John Iacovelli, the lighting by Martin Aronstein, the costumes by Jeanne Button, the sound by Jonathan Deans, and Arthur Gaffin was the production stage manager.

The world premiere of THE TWILIGHT OF THE GOLDS was presented by Theatre Corporation of America and Charles H. Duggan at the Pasadena Playhouse in Pasadena, California, on January 17, 1993. The cast and crew were the same with the following exceptions: The role of Suzanne was played by Jodi Thelen. The production was directed by Tom Alderman and the costumes were by Michael Abbott.

CHARACTERS

DAVID GOLD, late twenties. Charming, sensitive, gay, aspiring set designer. A fervent Wagner fan.

SUZANNE GOLD-STEIN, early thirties, his sister. Bright, attractive. Feels as if she never lived up to her own potential. Works as a buyer for Bloomingdale's department store.

ROB STEIN, early thirties, Suzanne's husband. A genetic researcher. A handsome, decent fellow. Still feels like an outsider in his wife's family.

PHYLLIS GOLD, fifties, David and Suzanne's mother. An elegant woman, smarter than she sometimes lets on. Perpetually worried about her children.

WALTER GOLD, fifties, David and Suzanne's father. A sometimes gruff New York businessman. Far more sensitive than he often appears.

TIME

Early autumn through late winter

PLACE

New York

A Note on the Production

This play can and should be presented in a variety of ways. What's important is for the designers to meet its challenges in the most creative and theatrical ways possible. This is, after all, a play told from the perspective of a young, ambitious set designer. Therefore, settings should be filled with theatrical tricks. The transformations from apartment to Wagnerian landscape should be seen as an opportunity for David to show off his scenic imagination (within the confines of the budget). The dichotomy between the modern apartment and the operatic surroundings should be both striking and humorous.

The lighting should perform a similar function. The designer should be encouraged to use the sky and its cloud formations to reflect the emotional progression of the drama. Some effects (fire, water) are specified in the script to underscore David's Wagnerian references and these should be created in the most magical ways possible. During David's Wagner story-telling, the lighting should take us subtly out of present time and into the mystical world of *The Ring* and then back again. The monologues, also, should be lit in a way that heightens their theatricality, these are arias, after all.

These guidelines are merely suggestions and are the result of what those of us involved in the original production learned about how this play works over the course of a year. The bottom line is all those involved should let their imaginations fly.

A Note on the Music

The excerpts used from the *Ring Cycle* should not include singing. When necessary, orchestral excerpt recordings should be used to avoid the use of voices which distract from the drama.

THE TWILIGHT OF THE GOLDS

Act I

Scene 1

AT RISE: The living room of a New York City apartment. It's the home of a young couple and is furnished in the style of a modular catalogue: tasteful, new, not particularly comfortable. A sofa, right, and two armchairs, left, form a triangle center, the left armchair can swivel around. In front of the chairs is a matching hassock which, when topped by a tray, doubles as a coffee table. Upstage left is a hallway that leads to the bedroom. Down right is a trunk with a cushion and down left is a leather reading chair with an ottoman footrest. Next to the reading chair is a small unit with a stereo, CD's and a three-dimensional replica of a strand of DNA. Medical journals can be seen on the chair and on a side table. Upstage left stands a rolling butcher block on which glasses and an ice bucket sit in preparation for guests.

The only LIGHT at first is from the New York City skyline seen through the upstage windows.

DAVID GOLD enters from the hallway and is lit by a SPOTLIGHT. HE addresses the audience and walks downstage.

DAVID. I'm one of those people who takes other people to the opera ... against their will. I estimate that since the age of fourteen, I've introduced more people to the Met than the good folks at Texaco. And every time, at a performance of *Bohème* or *Aida* or one of the other easy ones, as the chandeliers dimmed, I'd make the same joke. I'd say, "Now, try to enjoy it. It's all right if you don't. You're just here to find out if you have this particular genetic aberration." They usually didn't but they'd look adorable pretending they did. Anyway, I never imagined how that joke would come back to haunt me. (*HE sits on the trunk.*) I'm a set designer. At least in training. I wanted to design sets for Broadway starting when I was a kid and saw every show in town except *Oh, Calcutta* because you had to be eighteen or older. By the time I was old enough to see *Oh, Calcutta,* Broadway had lost its appeal: hardly any plays, and an audience of nothing but Japanese tourists and Hadassah ladies with husbands who spent the first fifteen minutes of Act I parking the Caddie. So, I embarked on a career in the Opera. I'm on the production staff at the Met. Which means I paint a lot of trees. But I figure, if you're going to work in an elitist art form that only a handful of people give a shit about, why not go all the way? And in opera, the composer's dead. So the designer can do something fabulous without getting a pissed off phone call from Arthur Miller's attorney. For instance ... (*LIGHTS up on the apartment. DAVID crosses upstage.*) ... here we have a smart looking Manhattan apartment. This is where my sister and her husband lived after they got married. Pages thirty through thirty-four of the Ikea catalogue. No real personality, but nothing objectionable.

This is where I saw my family together for the last time. Now, if this were an opera, and everything is, I'd do something spectacular. The Swiss designer, Appia, taught us that a good set is an image of how the characters view the world. Forget what's real, life is too short. (*HE sits in the swivel armchair.*) Take her away.

(*DAVID spins around and faces upstage. MUSIC: the prelude to* Götterdämmerung. *The LIGHTING changes and the rear wall of the living room flies slowly out of sight. Only the wall stage right with the front door remains. We now see the rest of the stage. At the rear and on the sides are huge rocky mountains. Upstage, the other FOUR CHARACTERS stand on a promontory in silhouette against the sky. The LIGHT comes up full as the MUSIC reaches its climax and DAVID addresses the audience.*)

DAVID. I was in a heavy Wagnerian phase at the time. Immersing myself in the *Ring Cycle* day and night. Pretty impressive, huh? It's a little too *Lost Horizon,* I know, but a lot more interesting than Ikea. This is how I like to picture what happened that stormy season, when I saw the last of the Golds. They would never understand, but to me, it's the perfect setting. Wagner put gods and goddesses on the stage looming on mountaintops in front of stormy skies. With miles of glorious music under them, they decide the fate of the world, not with magic and thunderbolts, but in domestic squabbles: conversations between husband and wife, brother and sister, parent and child.

(Upstage, the GOLD FAMILY join hands and descend from the promontory into the wings.)

DAVID. The Gold family, my nice family, had domestic squabbles and conversations, and we also decided the fate of the world. You'll see.

(SUZANNE GOLD STEIN enters, turns on a table LAMP and exits left to the kitchen.)

DAVID. It was my sister's anniversary and we had reservations for dinner. And she had a secret.

(HE exits through the door. SUZANNE reenters carrying a tray with cheese, crackers and cut vegetables. SHE stops by the stereo and hits a button. The MUSIC changes to soft "party" jazz. SHE then places the tray down on the hassock and looks at it.)

SUZANNE. *(Calling off.)* Rob? You know what we need? We need a cheese slicer. I always have to put out a knife. It's very low-class.

(ROB STEIN enters from the kitchen with a bowl of dip which HE puts down on the tray.)

ROB. It works just as good. Nobody notices.
SUZANNE. I can't understand why we don't have one. We must not have registered for it or something. Remind me to steal one the next time we're at my parents' house.
ROB. What'll they do when they entertain?

SUZANNE. Yeah, right. The last time they "entertained," David and I were brought downstairs at eight-thirty to sing *Matchmaker, Matchmaker* in feetie pajamas. We got paid in Godiva chocolates. (*SHE looks at the dip.*) What is that?

ROB. Dip. I said I'd take care of the dip. This is the dip.

SUZANNE. Honey, please tell me that's not Lipton Onion Soup mix and sour cream.

ROB. I went to a lot of trouble. I squeezed a lemon.

SUZANNE. It's like you're still in junior high school. I'm surprised you don't put out a tray of green M&M's and tell everybody they make you horny.

ROB. (*Grabs her by the waist and pulls her close.*) Wanna play "Seven Minutes in Heaven"?

SUZANNE. We don't have time.

ROB. Suzanne, it's just your parents and your brother.

SUZANNE. I'm sorry, but they're important.

ROB. I love it when you get that whiny kindergarten voice. It really turns me on.

SUZANNE. I'm sorry, but they made me what I am.

ROB. Thank God, I thought it was my fault.

SUZANNE. Schmuck.

(*THEY kiss.*)

ROB. Hello.

SUZANNE. Hello.

ROB. Happy anniversary.

SUZANNE. Happy anniversary, Doctor.

ROB. (*Looking at the DNA replica.*) Do you like the gift we got from Oxy?

SUZANNE. Ever so. I always wanted a three-dimensional chromosome in my living room. Why couldn't you work at Tiffany? (*SHE gathers magazines and CD's and puts them away.*)

ROB. Sorry. Dr. Lodge is brilliant but a bit socially challenged. How come we didn't get anything from your office?

SUZANNE. Because we're in Chapter Eleven. Can we not talk careers?

ROB. (*Takes a small Tiffany gift box from his pocket and prepares to give it to her.*) Fine. You want me to open some champagne? We've got some in the fridge.

SUZANNE. No, it makes me sleepy.

ROB. What are you talking about? It's a special occasion.

SUZANNE. I shouldn't drink.

ROB. You have your period?

SUZANNE. No. And I hate it when you ask me that.

ROB. What's eating you?

SUZANNE. I just don't want to drink.

(*The intercom BUZZER buzzes. ROB puts the gift back in his pocket and crosses to the front door where HE pushes a button on the speaker box. SUZANNE puts out coasters.*)

ROB. Hello?

PHYLLIS. (*Her voice through the intercom.*) Rob? Hi, sweetheart. We made it early, the traffic was light.

ROB. Good, I'll buzz you in.

SUZANNE. Mom?

PHYLLIS. Happy anniversary. Walter's parking the car. There was no traffic.

SUZANNE. I couldn't get an early reservation so we have time to kill.

PHYLLIS. Oh, that's all right. It'll be nice. Oh, you know who I saw at the beauty parlor this afternoon?

ROB. Can this wait till you come up in the elevator?

SUZANNE. Mom, come up.

PHYLLIS. What about your father?

ROB. I can buzz him in when he gets here.

PHYLLIS. Oh. All right. I'll just come up then. Okay.

SUZANNE. Apartment 22B.

(ROB presses the buzzer.)

SUZANNE. Don't be rude. *(SHE turns off the stereo.)*

(ROB shakes his head as HE ties his tie.)

SUZANNE. What?

ROB. Nothing.

SUZANNE. *What?*

ROB. Nothing. Why are you so nervous around them?

SUZANNE. I'm not nervous. I just had a very intense childhood. *(SHE crosses to him and straightens his tie.)*

ROB. Did they beat you?

SUZANNE. No. They *loved* me. We're a close family, it's a wonderful thing.

ROB. I'm not so sure. Reject your family before they reject you, that's what I always say.

SUZANNE. That's horrible. I like your parents. I think it's sweet that they're Orthodox. It gives them that charming, old-world, Amish quality.

(The intercom BUZZER buzzes. ROB pushes the button.)

ROB. Hello.
WALTER. *(Through the intercom.)* Hello?
ROB. Hello.
WALTER. Yeah, uh, uh, Rob?
ROB. Yes.
WALTER. Happy anniversary. I don't know what happened to your mother-in-law, I dropped her off.
ROB. Yeah, she's on her way up.
SUZANNE. Hi, Dad.
WALTER. Hi, Suzanne.

(The DOORBELL rings. ROB opens the door for PHYLLIS GOLD who enters, carrying a gift.)

WALTER. We made it here in no time. The traffic was nothing.
PHYLLIS. Your hallway always reeks of garlic, your neighbors must be loud.
ROB. Yeah, just come up.

(A SIREN is heard through the intercom. PHYLLIS and SUZANNE meet center and hug.)

WALTER. What? Wait a second, there's an ambulance going by.
SUZANNE. You look good.

PHYLLIS. I'm thinking of having my eyes done. You look stunning. The diet's working.

SUZANNE. This outfit, you can't see.

(SUZANNE takes Phyllis' wrap off left. PHYLLIS rearranges the pillows on the sofa.)

WALTER. It's amazing, the guys just stopped with the siren still going to buy a pretzel. I'd hate to be the poor *shlub* lying in the back.

ROB. It's a jungle down there. Come up here where it's nice.

PHYLLIS. Is that your father?

WALTER. Phyllis?

PHYLLIS. Walter, I'm up here. They did a good job. The apartment looks gorgeous.

WALTER. I can't wait to see it.

(SUZANNE reenters.)

PHYLLIS. (*Looking out where the windows used to be.*) And the view is stunning. It's clear today, you can see water.

WALTER. Really?

ROB. (*Desperate.*) Why don't I buzz you in?

WALTER. Okay.

SUZANNE. It's 22B.

WALTER. I remember. I'm not your mother.

(ROB presses the buzzer.)

PHYLLIS. (*Crossing to Rob, kissing him.*) I nearly got lost in the hall. Hi, Doctor Rob. Happy anniversary. Can you believe it's three years?

ROB. No. It feels like we spent twice that on the intercom.

PHYLLIS. I could cry. Oh, Rob, I read in the *Times* about those women suing Oxy over unsafe breast implants.

ROB. Right. Don't worry about it. Not my department.

PHYLLIS. You're not involved?

ROB. No, but I'm on the waiting list.

PHYLLIS. Oh, thank God. I got scared. But then I thought Oxy's so big, they must have good lawyers. Here, this is for the two of you. Mazel tov.

(*PHYLLIS hands SUZANNE the gift and sits. SUZANNE sits on the sofa and unwraps the present. ROB pours wine.*)

SUZANNE. Thanks. Nice paper.

ROB. Thanks, Mom.

SUZANNE. Uch. It's still weird when he calls you "Mom." It's like everyone has the same mother or you're all interchangeable.

PHYLLIS. I think it's nice.

ROB. I agree, Mom.

SUZANNE. Uch. Stop it. Any minute he's gonna give you his dirty laundry.

PHYLLIS. I wouldn't mind. Did David call?

SUZANNE. He'll be here. (*SHE takes out the gift: a glass table clock. SHE and ROB "Oooh" together.*) Ooh, it's pretty. Thanks, Ma.

PHYLLIS. Thank your father.

ROB. Thanks, Mom.

SUZANNE. You have the same one, don't you?

PHYLLIS. Yeah. You always liked it, so I figured it was safe.

(The DOORBELL rings)

SUZANNE. Ma, you're just making it easier for us to turn into you and Dad.

ROB. Your dream.

(ROB opens the door. WALTER GOLD enters, handing his coat to ROB.)

WALTER. Hey there, Rob. Looks like you're holding up pretty good.

ROB. Thanks.

WALTER. *(To Suzanne.)* There she is! *(Kissing her.)* Hiya, Suzy Q.

SUZANNE. You look fat.

WALTER. Kids. What a pleasure.

SUZANNE. We're eating at 7:30.

WALTER. *(Crossing to the sofa and the food, which HE eats continuously.)* Fine. Where are we going?

SUZANNE. Smith & Wollensky's. You said you wanted steaks.

WALTER. Good. That okay with you, Rob?

ROB. Whatever you want.

WALTER. What, where'd you want to go?

SUZANNE. He wanted to go for Thai food on Eighth Avenue.

WALTER. You know I can't eat that stuff with my stomach. Besides, it's your anniversary. You don't want to go to some greasy spoon on Eighth Avenue.

ROB. I just thought, I don't know, maybe, since it's where I proposed.

PHYLLIS. What? You're kidding.

ROB. That's where it happened. I put the ring around a piece of chicken satay. Suzanne's hand still smells of peanut sauce.

PHYLLIS. That's adorable. Suzanne, why didn't you tell us that story?

SUZANNE. I didn't want to give you the ammunition.

WALTER. (*Smiling, shaking his head.*) That's right. We're so terrible, you really got it rough. (*Looking at the chromosome.*) What the hell is that?

ROB. It's a replica of DNA.

PHYLLIS. A what?

SUZANNE. It's a gift from Oxy.

PHYLLIS. It's nice. Where are you putting it?

SUZANNE. It's being discussed.

PHYLLIS. Whatever—Oh, Denise Kaplan got engaged.

SUZANNE. Really?

PHYLLIS. To a dentist. Ugly as sin.

SUZANNE. Well, she's no beauty. She always had big teeth. Maybe that was the attraction.

PHYLLIS. You think she slept with him?

SUZANNE. Ma!

WALTER. What kind of question is that?

PHYLLIS. I'm just wondering.

SUZANNE. Of course she did. What are you imagining? She probably gives him great, toothy head.

ROB. Suzanne, you're so gross.

WALTER. That's the way you talk around your own parents?

SUZANNE. (*Smiling.*) You can handle it.

PHYLLIS. In my day, you didn't do that. Some world. See, years ago, if you got pregnant your life was over. Everyone was so petrified. Now, you have options.

SUZANNE. Which is better?

PHYLLIS. It's better now, sure. So how early do you think she slept with him?

SUZANNE. Ma.

ROB. Can we talk about something else?

WALTER. Hey, Phyllis, did you tell her who you saw at the beauty parlor?

PHYLLIS. Ooh, no. I saw Mrs. Reed.

SUZANNE. Really?

ROB. Who's that?

SUZANNE. My high school biology, physics, and chemistry teacher. She was amazing. That's why I got fives on the AP's.

WALTER. This dip is delicious.

ROB. Thank you. I made it.

WALTER. No kidding.

PHYLLIS. She always loved you, thought you were the greatest student.

WALTER. She was, Rob.

ROB. She told me.

PHYLLIS. She asked me if you were a surgeon yet. I told her what you were doing.

SUZANNE. What'd she say?

PHYLLIS. As long as you're happy.

SUZANNE. (*Moving away, angry.*) Why are you starting?

ROB. Don't get upset.

SUZANNE. You always have to make me feel bad.

WALTER. Sweetheart, your mother didn't mean it like that.

PHYLLIS. (*Defensive.*) No, she said you were probably smart, that the health-care system is such a shambles, you're better off. Honest.

SUZANNE. She was always a snob.

PHYLLIS. No, Suzanne, really, she was very down-to-earth. When I said you were a buyer for Bloomingdale's, she asked if you could get her a discount.

SUZANNE. You shouldn't tell anyone anything.

ROB. What are you so upset about? What are you ashamed of?

WALTER. We're all very proud of you.

SUZANNE. Will everyone lay off me? I'm not ashamed of anything. I've been out of that school for ten years, I don't care about those people anymore.

WALTER. All right. All right.

(*Pause.*)

SUZANNE. How did she look?

PHYLLIS. Good. The same. Teachers don't age.

SUZANNE. She'd probably like some of the jewelry we got in. Wait, I'll show you. (*SHE exits to the bedroom.*)

WALTER. Our little girl.

PHYLLIS. Did I say anything so terrible? She's so emotional. She gets that from you.

WALTER. (*Still eating.*) Rob, this dip is sensational.

ROB. Thanks, Dad.

SUZANNE. (*Entering.*) Uch. I wish he'd stop doing that. Here, this is all I have at home.

(*SHE hands PHYLLIS a small jewelry box. PHYLLIS opens it and takes out a gold ring. ROB joins WALTER on the sofa.*)

PHYLLIS. Oh, this is stunning.

SUZANNE. It's a copy of Paloma Picasso.

PHYLLIS. Really. It's a little like Denise Kaplan's engagement ring.

ROB. That tramp.

PHYLLIS. Walter, look. It's a stunning ring. Fake?

WALTER. Gotta be. Nobody can afford real jewelry anymore. Everybody's dying.

ROB. How's your business?

WALTER. Not bad. Pearson's indestructible. Why? (*Reaching for his wallet.*) You need money?

ROB. No. Just wondering.

WALTER. We're okay. (*Rising.*) Pearson will always hang on because we're good at what we do. People give us their money to invest and they use our credit cards because we provide what they're looking for: the appearance if not the reality of financial security.

SUZANNE. Dad, you're scaring me.

WALTER. Don't worry. Phyllis, just keep looking at the fake stuff.

PHYLLIS. (*Still with the ring.*) You think I should get one?

SUZANNE. No, it's cheaply made. See that? That's the trouble with my job, I get too much information about the product. There's always some reason not to buy. It's taken all the fun out of shopping.

ROB. You manage.

PHYLLIS. Well, with some things, you just have to go with your feelings.

(There is a KNOCK at the door. SUZANNE is frightened.)

SUZANNE. Gimme ... *(SHE takes the ring from her mother, puts it back in the case, and places it in a drawer.)*

PHYLLIS. What?

WALTER. What's the matter?

SUZANNE. Shush!

ROB. *(Rising.)* Honey, maybe it's David.

SUZANNE. *(Whispering.)* He has a key.

PHYLLIS. *(To Rob.)* Didn't you pay the rent?

SUZANNE. Shh.

(There is a tense silence.)

DAVID. *(Opening the door with his key.)* Hello? Anybody home?

SUZANNE. David! Oh, thank God it's you.

(DAVID enters carrying a small shopping bag. SUZANNE hugs him.)

DAVID. I get that whenever I enter a room. Hi. Happy anniversary. Hi, Mom, Dad. Rob, congratulations. We're counting on you to stick this out.

SUZANNE. Shut up. We've got a while before dinner

DAVID. I hope it's Thai. I know a great place on Eighth Avenue.

SUZANNE. (*Warning him to drop the subject.*) I asked you nice.

WALTER. Hey, he looks good.

DAVID. Why didn't you open the door when I knocked?

ROB. She's just paranoid. David, there are drinks over there.

DAVID. (*Crossing to the bar, looking at Walter.*) Thanks. You look fat. (*HE takes off his coat and pours himself some wine.*)

SUZANNE. I'm not paranoid. Three weeks ago, Mrs. Fleischer on the top floor opened her door to see who was knocking and this man burst in and threw her against the wall, screaming at her, calling her a rich bitch.

PHYLLIS. That's awful.

SUZANNE. He just kept yelling, "You fucking rich bitch, I should kill you."

WALTER. Did he take anything?

SUZANNE. No. He just smashed stuff. And the weirdest part of it was that he knew the names of everything.

DAVID, PHYLLIS, AND WALTER. What?

SUZANNE. Brand names. He mentioned Waterford Crystal, Wedgewood China, and Levolor Blinds.

PHYLLIS. He has good taste.

DAVID. A bit unimaginative. Did he mention Sidney Poitier?

SUZANNE. It's not funny.

WALTER. Well, you want to move? I thought this was a good neighborhood.

ROB. There's no such thing anymore.

SUZANNE. We're not gonna move. It's just frightening, that's all.

PHYLLIS. Did anyone tell the police?

SUZANNE. Yes. They said the best thing to do was not to let anyone in unless they buzzed through the intercom and you know exactly who they are.

DAVID. That's neighborly. You'll never meet the people across the hall.

ROB. This is New York. You don't actually see your neighbors until they're on the cover of the *Post*.

DAVID. Maybe this guy's a messenger, sent to teach us all a lesson about materialism.

SUZANNE. Yeah, right. What'd you bring me?

DAVID. Ah. The gift of a lifetime.

SUZANNE. Gimme.

(HE takes out a yellow Tower Records bag and removes a boxed set of CD's.)

SUZANNE. Oh, not again. I hate it when you do this.

WALTER. What is it?

DAVID. This is Wilhelm Furtwängler's recording of Richard Wagner's complete *Ring of the Nibelung*. It's the most fascinating work of art man has ever produced. Happy anniversary.

ROB. *(Taking the CD's and crossing to the stereo.)* Thanks, David. We'll put it with the others.

SUZANNE. He always does this. He keeps bringing us CD's of opera and old musicals. It's so rude. He knows we don't have any interest.

DAVID. Why are you so closed to everything?

SUZANNE. I'm not closed, I'm discriminating. Just because you like something doesn't mean everyone else has to.

PHYLLIS. Suzanne, try to be appreciative. David, give me a kiss.

(DAVID and PHYLLIS meet center and kiss.)

DAVID. You look good, Ma. You shouldn't get any work done.

PHYLLIS. See? He's sweet.

SUZANNE. Fine, you listen to the *Ring of the Niblicks*.

DAVID. I'm just trying to enrich your lives. And I have a friend at Tower, so I get everything real cheap. Someday, you or your children will sit down and listen to this stuff and be transported to new heights.

SUZANNE. Someone, make him stop.

DAVID. (*Grandly.*) You know, Suzanne, I think you're afraid. You're afraid of your own soul that hungers for life at a higher pitch.

SUZANNE. Whatever. Thanks.

DAVID. Besides, that's not your real gift. I knew you'd throw a hissy fit. Here. Happy anniversary. (*HE pulls a small gift box out of the same bag and hands it to her.*)

SUZANNE. Ooh. What is it?

DAVID. It's a cheese slicer. I didn't think you had one. (*HE looks at the knife sticking out of the cheese.*)

SUZANNE. Thank you, we didn't. You're so smart.

(SUZANNE opens the box and holds the slicer up. The FAMILY "Oohs." DAVID conducts them louder.)

DAVID. The handle is crystal. The lady at Fortunoff's said the third anniversary is crystal and glass.

PHYLLIS. Oh, I got it right and I didn't even know.

DAVID. That's the modern gift. She couldn't remember the traditional. But I figured you're a modern couple.

SUZANNE. It's beautiful. I love you. You have the best taste.

DAVID. Well, I buy nothing but Wedgewood China and Levolor Blinds. Use it in good health.

WALTER. So, how ya doin', kiddo? You look great. Doesn't he look great?

PHYLLIS. He's too thin.

WALTER. He's not too thin. Look at his arms. He's strong. (*HE squeezes David's arm.*)

DAVID. Well, I've moved up to a heavier drafting pencil.

WALTER. So, when are you gonna come play tennis with me?

DAVID. Dad, you're a demon on the court. I wouldn't have a chance.

WALTER. Rob played with me last weekend.

ROB. That's right, Dad.

SUZANNE. Uch. Cut that out.

DAVID. (*Sitting in the reading chair.*) I've been busy. Soon. So, guys, three years, huh? Stephen sends his regards. He would have come but he wasn't invited.

PHYLLIS. Now, David, come on, that's not right.

SUZANNE. You know you could have brought him. I just thought ...

WALTER. (*Rising.*) Hey, what time is it? Rob, do you know what's happening in the game? Is there a TV in your room?

ROB. Yeah, sure.

(WALTER walks with ROB to the bedroom. DAVID turns away and kicks off his shoes.)

WALTER. I just gotta check the score.

(Pause.)

DAVID. Sorry.

PHYLLIS. Look, that's all right.

DAVID. No it's not, I just lost twenty bucks.

SUZANNE. You and Stephen make bets on how we'll behave? That's disgusting.

DAVID. Hey, I took your side.

PHYLLIS. Give it time.

DAVID. I know, I know. I'm one of the lucky ones.

PHYLLIS. So, how are you, really?

DAVID. What? I'm fine.

PHYLLIS. Yeah? Then why are you so thin?

SUZANNE. You have lost weight, David.

DAVID. (*Rising, crossing right.*) Will you stop it? Please, I've lost a few pounds. I can't wait for the day when I can lose weight or catch a cold without everyone planning what to read at the memorial.

PHYLLIS. Oh, God forbid.

SUZANNE. David!

DAVID. I'm sorry. I came from a funeral.

SUZANNE. Whose?

DAVID. A friend of mine, a baritone. (*HE sits facing Phyllis.*) Mom, you saw him last year in *The Magic Flute.* With the feathers.

PHYLLIS. (*Gasps.*) You're kidding. He was gorgeous.

DAVID. Don't you know? We all are.

PHYLLIS. That's true. They stay young. It's because they don't have children. So he slept around? Mmm.

SUZANNE. (*Sits next to David on the sofa.*) Stephen could have come.

DAVID. Yeah, that's all right. We've been having problems.

SUZANNE. Sexual?

PHYLLIS. I don't what to hear it. Your generation thinks of nothing but.

DAVID. No, not sexual. The sex is fabulous.

PHYLLIS. Really? I don't want to hear it.

DAVID. It's just tense. He says I force my interests on him.

SUZANNE. You?

DAVID. He says I'm like a Jewish mother pushing food on a militant anorexic.

(*HE and SUZANNE turn to Phyllis.*)

PHYLLIS. What are you looking at me for?

DAVID. We're coming up on our third anniversary too.

PHYLLIS. Of what?

DAVID. Mom, don't be mean. I said you don't need a face-lift. (*Eating a celery stick with Rob's dip.*) Uch. This is Lipton's.

SUZANNE. Here, I'll finish it.

PHYLLIS. Suzanne, don't eat from his mouth.

SUZANNE. Mom. (*Bites the other end of the celery stick and puts the rest away in a napkin.*)

PHYLLIS. So, what, are you gonna break off with him?

DAVID. I hope not. I really can't face dating again.

(*PHYLLIS rises and crosses upstage.*)

DAVID. I feel lonely sometimes.

SUZANNE. I worry about you.

DAVID. I know you do.

SUZANNE. We should go out more, the four of us.

DAVID. I know we should. But Stephen thinks Rob is homophobic.

SUZANNE. He is not. Just because his parents think you're an abomination doesn't mean he does.

DAVID. Thank you.

SUZANNE. People don't automatically think the way their parents do. It's not fair to ...

DAVID. Suzanne, don't worry about it, Stephen thinks everybody is homophobic. Including me. So, what about you, Anniversary Girl? How's it going?

SUZANNE. I'm good. We're good.

DAVID. Yeah?

SUZANNE. Yeah.

DAVID. I'm glad.

PHYLLIS. It's so beautiful the way you two get along. I'm *kvelling*. I guess I did something right.

SUZANNE. Mom, you did everything right.

PHYLLIS. Yeah, sure.

SUZANNE. I've got a surprise.

DAVID. What?

SUZANNE. An announcement. Big one. Rob doesn't know.

DAVID. You little minx. What is it?

PHYLLIS. Oh, thank God, you're going back to medical school.

SUZANNE. No. And why do you have to say things like that?

DAVID. Mother, behave or we'll put you in a home.

(WALTER and ROB enter, talking baseball.)

WALTER. Lousy Mets. Same thing every year.

ROB. They'll be back.

WALTER. It's so aggravating.

DAVID. *(Crossing to Walter.)* Dad, we should go to a game together. When's helmet day?

WALTER. You hate baseball.

DAVID. I do. But I love those little helmets.

PHYLLIS. How's your job, David?

SUZANNE. Are you making any money?

DAVID. Suzanne, I'm an artist.

WALTER. That means no.

DAVID. Don't worry about me. I'm working my way up in an art form that is dearly loved by very rich people.

WALTER. Just hope they can hold on to their money.

DAVID. That's your job, Dad.

PHYLLIS. What are you working on now?

SUZANNE. Mom, don't get him started.

DAVID. *(Crosses to the stereo and picks up the* Ring *CD's.)* Wagner's *Ring Cycle*, day and night.

SUZANNE. I thought he was an anti-Semite.

DAVID. That's a simplification. Wagner might have had Jewish blood.

PHYLLIS. Jewish anti-Semites, they're the worst.

ROB. What's it about?

SUZANNE. Oh, God. Wake me up when it's over.

PHYLLIS. Suzanne, listen to your brother.

WALTER. You'll like this, it's about jewelry. It's about a gold ring that everybody fights for. And for that you gotta sit for a week.

DAVID. Twenty-two hours with intermissions.

ROB. That's worse than Rosh Hashanah.

WALTER. Nothing's worse than Rosh Hashanah.

DAVID. And it's not about a ring. Not just a ring. It's about everything. Life, love, civilization, evolution. It's amazing. This twisted little anti-Semite with bad skin and B.O. created a work of art that is as unfathomable as the Bible.

WALTER. He talks so dramatic.

DAVID. Let me give you an example. The last scene of *Die Walküre*. Wotan, the head god, is angry at his daughter, Brünnhilde, because she defied his wishes.

ROB. What'd she do?

DAVID. If I answer that, we'll never eat. Just go with me. Brünnhilde is Wotan's favorite child, she is the living embodiment of his will.

PHYLLIS. He speaks so beautifully, doesn't he? Remember in junior high ...

DAVID. Ma! But she has disobeyed him. Wotan has no choice but to punish her by taking away her godhead.

SUZANNE. Her what?

DAVID. (*Hops up and sits on the back of the sofa.*) He makes her a mortal woman. He puts her to sleep and lays her down on a rock surrounded by magic fire. Brünnhilde will rest there until a hero brave enough to walk through that fire can wake her.

(As HE speaks, the sky behind him starts to flicker and then becomes engulfed with beautiful RED FLAMES. This is the "Magic Fire" and the MUSIC from this scene can be heard softly in the background.)

DAVID. A hero who knows nothing of fear and obeys only Nature's law. A hero who is strong enough and courageous enough to truly love. Wotan knows too well that he will never see his child again. He kisses her on the forehead and says, "Farewell, you valiant, glorious child!" Forced into obeying laws that he no longer understands or believes in, this god must abandon what he loves most of all. In one moment, with fire sweeping through the sky, we see parent and child, god and mortal, parting ways for eternity. And we know that it could be no other way.

(The FIRE and MUSIC fade away. Pause.)

PHYLLIS. Doesn't he speak beautifully?

SUZANNE. When he explains it, it sounds interesting.

WALTER. Meanwhile, it takes five and a half hours to get to that scene.

DAVID. Nine if you count *Rheingold*.

ROB. We should go. See it once.

SUZANNE. Have fun. I would never make it, I slept through *Dances With Wolves*. Either that or I'd start laughing uncontrollably like Mary at Chuckles' funeral.

DAVID. (*Sinking down to join her on the sofa.*) "A little song, a little dance ..."

SUZANNE and DAVID. "... a little seltzer down your pants."

(*THEY laugh together.*)

ROB. What are you talking about?

WALTER. What is that?

DAVID and SUZANNE. *Mary Tyler Moore Show*.

SUZANNE. When Chuckles the Clown dies, and Mary can't stop laughing at his funeral.

WALTER. Eighty thousand dollars in education between them and they still communicate through sit-com re-runs. Can you imagine?

PHYLLIS. (*Still hooked.*) How does it end, David? I don't remember?

DAVID. The *Ring*?

SUZANNE. Ma, wasn't one bad enough?

PHYLLIS. Come on, tell us. I'm interested.

DAVID. Very simple. The end of everything as we know it. The world has become corrupt and lazy. It seems that mortals lie, cheat, and steal even worse than the gods did. True love is destroyed as people cling to twisted ideas of honor and duty that are based on lies. Brünnhilde's hero, Siegfried is murdered. Inconsolable, and seeing how the world is turning to shit, she erects a giant funeral pyre.

(*HE rises. Again, the FLAMES appear faintly in the sky behind him and we hear the MUSIC from the "Immolation Scene."*)

DAVID. There is no point in preserving this failed civilization. Brünnhilde sacrifices herself and all that is in the hope that something better may emerge. She calls up to Wotan, sitting powerless in his castle in the sky, *"Ruhe, ruhe, du Gott!"* Rest, rest, O God! She mounts her horse and jumps into the fire. The flames rise to consume everything in sight, including the castle of the gods. (*The image of WATER replaces the flames.*) And then, the mighty river overflows its banks and sweeps away all the wreckage, covering everything and everyone with a great flood of rebirth and new potential. Finally, as the water sinks back to its natural level, a few dazed survivors appear to behold the brave new world that stands before them. It's up to them now. And it's up to us what to make of it.

(*The WATER image disappears. The MUSIC fades away. There is a slight pause.*)

PHYLLIS. Beautiful.

DAVID. That's just a rough idea. There's a lot more to it than that. I left out the dragon and the dwarfs. You can see how it's fun to work on.

WALTER. What was that German?

DAVID. *"Ruhe, ruhe, du Gott."* Rest, rest, God, your work is done.

WALTER. Here translate this: *"Es, es, shane, Gott in Himmel."* *Faschtaste?*

DAVID. I only speak opera German. What does it mean?

WALTER. It's Yiddish for "Eat, eat, for God's sake!" Can we go yet?

SUZANNE. Just a few more minutes. We're not getting there early so you can schmooze the maitre d'. (*SHE starts to clear the food away.*)

ROB. David, you know, it sounds really interesting.

SUZANNE. It does?

ROB. We talk about this stuff constantly at Oxy.

DAVID. Opera?

ROB. No, of course not. No, the idea of a post-Natural epoch. We talk about the role of our research in evolutionary history. What *we* do now that God is resting.

PHYLLIS. He's either resting or in a coma.

ROB. We're very close to releasing some historic technology.

WALTER. I'm glad to hear it. Thank God.

DAVID. Why are you so happy?

WALTER. I bought some Oxy stock. Bio-technology is a big field. You've got to watch health trends. You know, I could have bought shares in a company making condoms in 1983, didn't take it. Can you imagine, with all that's happened? Can you imagine?

SUZANNE. Dad, that's sick.

ROB. Why? Look, if lives are saved, it's okay if somebody makes a buck.

WALTER. Exactly.

ROB. The government isn't helping anymore. So now, whatever we come up with in the labs has to be something with profit potential. Which also means we have to be protective of any discoveries. That's what's holding up the new big thing.

DAVID. What's the "new big thing"?

ROB. I'm not supposed to talk about it.

DAVID. You just did.

ROB. I really shouldn't.

SUZANNE. David, you don't want him to lose his job.

DAVID. Come on. What, I'm going to steal Oxy Co.'s big discovery and start cloning people in my kitchenette? I'm just interested in the abstract.

ROB. All right. But it's not to leave this room. It looks like the Human Genome Project is a lot further along than everybody thinks.

PHYLLIS. Really. What's that?

ROB. Basically, what I'm saying is that we've finally developed advanced procedures for individual gene identification. Including a way to do these tests through amniocentesis at the end of the first trimester.

DAVID. Which means?

ROB. The possibilities are endless. Think about it. This is an unbelievable breakthrough. It opens new doors. Unfortunately, it will be a while before the public knows about it because, typically, we're fighting in court over the patents.

WALTER. Patents? On the equipment?

ROB. On the genes.

DAVID. You still didn't answer my question. What does it mean?

ROB. What, you mean practical applications?

DAVID. That'd be good.

SUZANNE. Don't be snotty.

ROB. Curing genetic diseases for one. There are people walking around with these ticking time bombs in their DNA waiting to go off. By locating the gene, we're ten times closer to a cure.

PHYLLIS. I had a friend, remember Gloria Myers? Her mother had Huntington's.

ROB. Perfect example.

PHYLLIS. I used to go to her house. Her mother couldn't walk or eat by herself. She kept having these hysterics, wanting to speak, to communicate somehow, and just being defeated by her body. Finally, she gave up.

WALTER. Terrible thing.

PHYLLIS. And everywhere you looked in that house there were reminders of what she was like before. Pictures, paintings the mother used to do, the piano she used to play. I knew it was killing Gloria. Not only seeing her mother fall apart that way, but knowing that the same thing could happen to her. Can you imagine, feeling like you're looking at your own future that way? Just awful, her mother. You've never seen anyone look so terrible.

DAVID. I have.

(A short pause.)

SUZANNE. How is Gloria? What happened to her?

PHYLLIS. We lost touch. I don't remember why.

WALTER. Very sad.

DAVID. *(Back to business.)* There's more to it, isn't there?

ROB. What do you mean?

DAVID. All that genetic decoding. That's dangerous stuff.

WALTER. What dangerous? Is anybody else starving to death?

ROB. Sure, there are going to be ethical questions. Who is privy to the information? The insurance companies? The government? Things like that will be argued case by case until we can come up with some sort of standards.

DAVID. What about the amniocentesis?

ROB. What about it?

DAVID. Why'd you mention it? What are you going to do with it?

ROB. Simple. By having the information available before birth, you'll determine what problems or abnormalities may be present in the fetus. Doctors can be ready for any emergencies. And the parents can be trained to help the child overcome any behavioral pre-dispositions.

WALTER. We could have taught Suzanne to hate shopping.

ROB. Later on, by using this information, we can develop ways to correct or reverse the genes.

PHYLLIS. Maybe they could give me a sense of direction.

ROB. That's years away. Until then, in tragic scenarios, the parents and doctors may choose to terminate the pregnancy.

DAVID. On what grounds?

ROB. I told you. At first, as with anything, it will be on a case by case basis.

DAVID. I don't believe this. Do you people have any idea how dangerous this is?

SUZANNE. I thought you were pro-choice.

ROB. Look, David, we are, in effect, on the verge of creating a better world. That's what science is—the pursuit of a better world, one that minimizes misery.

DAVID. Whose? Face it, Rob, this is Eugenics. It's blatant Nazi philosophy.

ROB. (*Rises.*) Oh, here we go. Every time there's the slightest scientific advance, some knee-jerk liberals start shouting about Nazis. We are trying to make life better. You should hear Dr. Lodge speak. He's truly eloquent on the subject.

DAVID. Lodge? Dr. Adrian Lodge?

ROB. You know him?

DAVID. I saw him on *Night-Line*.

PHYLLIS. He's very distinguished.

DAVID. For a Nazi.

ROB. The man is at the top of his field.

DAVID. (*Rising, crossing to Rob.*) Rob, how can you buy into this? You're a Jew. Your parents are Orthodox, for God's sake.

ROB. Yes, I'm a Jew, so I'm wary of political evil masquerading as science. Absolutely. But I don't see politics here.

DAVID. Oh, come on.

ROB. And, as a Jew, I believe in the value of knowledge, the rewards of study. Period.

SUZANNE. Is this really how we want to spend our anniversary?

ROB. Knowledge is neutral. It simply is. It's what bad people do with that knowledge that's dangerous.

DAVID. It's good people that scare me.

(*HE crosses back to the reading chair and puts on his shoes. ROB follows him.*)

ROB. David, do me a favor. Imagine a world without Huntington's disease. One where that woman's mother can still play the piano. That's what we're working towards. A world without needless suffering.

DAVID. Okay, I get it. I imagine a world without critics.

ROB. I'm being serious.

DAVID. So am I. I imagine a world without critics. A brave new world without John Simon. (*HE crosses right.*) But then that's also a world without George Bernard Shaw. You can't lose one without the other.

WALTER. Have you been to the theatre lately? We already live in a world without George Bernard Shaw.

PHYLLIS. Someone at the beauty parlor was talking about women who had abortions because they found out they were having girls and they wanted boys.

DAVID. What about that?

ROB. A world with more boys, you'd love that.

SUZANNE. Rob, don't.

(*Pause. DAVID smiles. ROB turns away, embarrassed.*)

DAVID. Well, yeah, maybe I would. But it's not our place to create. We have enough problems of our own.

ROB. You don't under ...

PHYLLIS. (*Stands and interrupts the argument.*) I have faith in people. They'll make the right decision most of the time. Especially in this country. On the whole, I think people are good.

WALTER. Aww, isn't that beautiful?

DAVID. Yes. Thank you, Anne Frank.

PHYLLIS. Fine, make fun of me. But I mean it. I believe in the family of man.

DAVID. What about our friend who likes to smash Wedgewood china and yell at Mrs. Fleischer?

PHYLLIS. If given a chance, an education, and love, he could come home to the family of man.

WALTER. I'm getting the coats. (*Exits to the bedroom.*)

ROB. Look, David, I understand how you feel. Sometimes I wish we could get out of the way and let Nature take over, like in the opera. But in reality, Nature fails. You have no idea what horrific defects can strike a person, and now we can find out before they embark on a tragic life. We have the technology, we're going to have more and more information. There's no going back. Why force someone through an unhappy existence? Not to mention their family. Let's give people the choice. Let each family do what's right. It's nobody else's business, not the government's, not some religious crackpot's, not even the doctor's. (*Crossing to David.*) Just last week, a woman at New York Hospital found out that her fetus had a tumor the size of a baseball on the tailbone. If it was benign, the doctors would have to remove it and the kid would have no legs or backside. If it was malignant, the kid would die. That's Nature, David. That's God's work, but now we have the ability to head it off at the pass.

(*SUZANNE cries out, obviously agitated. WALTER reenters with the coats. PHYLLIS and DAVID cross upstage towards her.*)

SUZANNE. Oh, God, can we please stop this? I can't take it anymore. This conversation is so horrible.

WALTER. What?

PHYLLIS. Suzanne, what is it?
ROB. Suzanne?
DAVID. You need a drink?
SUZANNE. No. I'm pregnant.

(A slight pause. And then, the scene is transformed to one of complete joy. PHYLLIS screams with delight. As the GOLDS hug each other and celebrate, ROB slowly sits down on the trunk.)

PHYLLIS. I knew it! You said you had a surprise. I didn't want to jinx it!
WALTER. My little girl! Congratulations, Rob.
DAVID. Well, it's about time. I was born to be an uncle.
ROB. When did you find out?
SUZANNE. (*Crossing to Rob.*) Yesterday.
ROB. And you didn't tell me?
SUZANNE. I wanted to tell everybody together at dinner. But then, I got so upset with all that talk about ...
PHYLLIS. (*Rushing over and covering Suzanne's ears.*) No, don't think about it, don't think about it, don't think about it.
DAVID. Congratulations, sis.
WALTER. Hey, speaking of dinner, come on, let's go already.

(THEY prepare to leave.)

SUZANNE. Are you happy, Rob?

(The OTHERS turn to hear his reply.)

ROB. Of course I am. Are you crazy?

WALTER. Hey, Rob, you want to call your parents before we leave?

ROB. No, it's the Shabbas, they won't answer the phone.

PHYLLIS. Oh, that's a shame. This is such a beautiful moment.

WALTER. That's right, Grandma.

PHYLLIS. Shut up.

WALTER. This is what life is all about. The family together, everybody healthy, good news to share.

DAVID. (*Joining his parents in an embrace.*) We're very lucky people.

WALTER. That's for sure. When this goes, we're really in trouble. Come on. (*WALTER ushers PHYLLIS out the door.*)

ROB. We're late.

DAVID. You know, Stephen's and my anniversary is in six months. So, I guess you'll all be at our house.

SUZANNE. (*On her way out.*) David!

DAVID. Who knows? Maybe I'll be pregnant.

(*THEY are gone except for ROB who lingers for a moment. SUZANNE enters downstage right from the wings, watching the scene. ROB puts on his coat, gathers his strength and follows the others out.*)

Scene 2

SUZANNE sits and addresses the audience.

SUZANNE. I should have told him first. "Shoulda, woulda, coulda." Do you get points for at least knowing when you should have done something? Do I get partial credit for guilt? I should have stayed in ballet class. I should have invited Margo the handicapped girl to my bat mitzvah. I should have been a doctor. That's a biggie. I had the interest, had the grades. But I hate being tested. My heart starts pounding and my hands sweat. You can't get an M.D. if you hate being tested, so I switched to marketing. My parents were devastated. They said I always take the easy way out. I guess I do, I married Rob. No, I take that back. There's nothing wrong with Rob. My name was Gold, his was Stein, if I married him I'd be Goldstein, it made Jewish sense. You should have seen him in college. Rob was amazing, really passionate about everything, like he didn't know it was the Eighties. When he chose research over a medical practice, I thought it was so noble, so sexy. I didn't think how much less he'd be making than the average anesthesiologist. I take that back, too. God, why do I do that? I love Rob. I couldn't live without him. I tried. Five years ago. We had been together *forever* and I decided enough was enough. I needed to find myself and reach my potential. Dr. Rob was a symbol of everything wrong with my life. So, I walked. (*SHE rises.*) It was exhilarating at first. On the go in the big city. Got a new outlook, a new self-image. I was ready to start dating. (*Beat.*) Uch, how do people do this? I would go with women from work to bars and then go home and cry my eyes out. I'm sorry, I am not equipped to sit in some yuppie watering hole with my tits sticking out and appear interested in some M.B.A. with thinning hair telling Ivan Boesky jokes. But, I didn't give up. I took control of my life and I went, I swear to God, to a computer dating service. Data Dates. On Lexington. Isn't that embarrassing? I met with this perky woman named Jan who still had a Dorothy Hammill haircut which I thought was rather odd. She told me they have a large base of subscribers who pay yearly until they find their "life mate," that's what she said, "life mate." It sounded like something on *Nova*. They take down all this information and then they put you on a video. There's a library that has books of pictures of the people available and then you can watch the ones who interest you on TV. "Well, Jan, that sounds very high tech," I said, which made her even perkier. "Oh, Suzanne, I really want to see this work for you. Are you committed? Tell me you are and we'll get started right away." It was very seductive, you know, in a Jews for Jesus kind of way. And then I asked about the money. "Suzanne, don't let the money stop you. We'll work it out." "But, how much is it?" Okay, it was thirty-five hundred dollars for the first six months and twenty-two fifty after that. I said, "Excuse me?" And then Jan tossed her Dorothy Hammill hair to one side and said, "I know it sounds like a lot. Let me talk to my supervisor." By this point, my heart was pounding like during the S.A.T.'s, so I slipped out of Jan's office and ran down the hall to the elevator. And there on the left, was the library. I knew I wasn't supposed to go in, I wasn't "committed," but I couldn't resist, I had to see. I opened the eligible man book and tried not to hyperventilate. (*Beat.*) How can I describe to you what I saw? The best I can do is: think *WKRP in Cincinatti*. Without the cute one. I almost paid over five thousand dollars to have dinner with Les Nesman. God, how dare these people take advantage of our needs that way. Especially in a desperate era like this one. I ran home and cried my eyes out. Were these really my options—whining Wharton graduates or "dating cults"? Or being alone? It was multiple choice and I never felt so unprepared. I just wanted to crawl under a rock and go to sleep for thirty years. I called Rob immediately.

(ROB enters through the front door.)

SUZANNE. Two months later, we were engaged.

(LIGHTS up on the apartment. ROB looks out the door, saying goodbye to the Golds.)

ROB. No, the elevator's that way, Mom.
PHYLLIS. *(Offstage.)* They're still with the cooking next door.
ROB. David, grab your mother. Good night.

(The GOLDS ad lib "Good nights" as ROB closes and triple-locks the door.)

SUZANNE. You're mad.
ROB. Why didn't you tell me? How could you not tell me?
SUZANNE. I thought it would be nice if you all found out together.

ROB. (*Sitting.*) I can't believe you. You're having a child with your husband. You acted like you were bringing home your report card! I felt like I was totally out of the loop. You didn't even look at me when you said it. I was waiting for your father to ask me what my involvement was. It was humiliating.

SUZANNE. I thought we would celebrate now just the two of us but I guess that's out of the question.

ROB. Just this once, Suzanne, I should have been more important. You're going to have to decide, once and for all—it's them or me. I am sick of being married to Brenda Potemkin.

SUZANNE. Who?

ROB. The spoiled princess in *Goodbye Columbus*.

SUZANNE. That's my parents' favorite movie.

ROB. No kidding.

SUZANNE. Rob, stop it. You are the most important person in my life. I live with you, don't I?

ROB. That's not enough and you know it.

SUZANNE. (*Crosses to him and kisses him.*) I promise. You can have my undivided attention up until the baby is born.

ROB. I'm doomed.

SUZANNE. I love you.

(*THEY kiss. HE softens and takes her in his arms.*)

SUZANNE. Rob?

ROB. What?

SUZANNE. Do you think we're ready for this?

ROB. More than most. Yeah. I think in some ways, it's just what we need.

SUZANNE. Me too.

ROB. If it will make you happy for once.

SUZANNE. The timing is right, don't you think?

ROB. I guess.

SUZANNE. I think it's a good time. The apartment is finished. (*Looking around.*) Well, close enough.

ROB. It looks fine.

SUZANNE. (*Rising.*) So, what are you hoping for? Boy or girl? I can't wait to find out so we can start painting.

ROB. We don't have to.

SUZANNE. What?

ROB. We don't have to wait. I can talk to Dr. Lodge. We can get an amniocentesis at Oxy. The new one.

SUZANNE. God. Really?

ROB. We should test for Tay-Sachs anyway.

SUZANNE. Isn't it too early?

ROB. No. Not for us. Adrian is always saying we need more subjects for study. We can do it in a couple of weeks. Consider it a perk. Which is another reason you should have told me first.

SUZANNE. I'm sorry.

ROB. God forbid there's anything wrong, we could have taken care of it without everybody knowing. Now, God forbid, it would be a mess.

SUZANNE. Rob, are you crazy? You think I could go through something like that without telling my parents?

ROB. No, of course not. You can't fart without telling your parents.

SUZANNE. Rob! Why are you being so mean to me? I'm a pregnant woman, I'm not in my right mind. I'm very fragile!

ROB. Is this what I have to look forward to?

SUZANNE. I'm in hormone hell.

ROB. I always thought pregnant women were really sexy.

SUZANNE. Yeah? You want to do something about it?

ROB. Maybe. But shouldn't you call your folks first?

SUZANNE. No. They're not home yet. Rob, I was scared. I wanted to rally the troops.

ROB. You don't have to, you know that. If you just let me in ...

SUZANNE. I know.

ROB. (*Stands and hugs Suzanne.*) We're gonna be fine. This is a good thing.

SUZANNE. You mean it?

ROB. I'm telling you.

SUZANNE. I don't call my parents when I fart.

ROB. Uh-huh.

(*HE pulls the Tiffany gift box from his pocket and gives it to her. SUZANNE gasps and buries her head in his chest. HE leads her toward the bedroom as WALTER enters from the wings downstage left and watches them.*)

ROB. Can I talk to Dr. Lodge? He'll be more than happy to do it.

SUZANNE. It's so frightening. Maybe we should wait.

ROB. Look, I'm sure it's okay. Why take a chance? It's just information.

(*THEY exit.*)

Scene 3

WALTER addresses the audience.

WALTER. I went to the doctor the other day because my stomach was being a little too sensitive to the Dow Industria" Average. Sometimes I think they should use my bowel movements as a major economic indicator. Anyway, I was stuck sitting in the waiting room, amazing how those guys get away with that, and I started reading one of those *People*-type magazines. They had a ten page spread on all these Hollywood stars who are coming out now and saying they were physically and emotionally abused by their parents. Can you imagine? My mother is seventy-eight years old, I would be afraid to say something like that in private, never mind in a magazine. She would come to my office and bash my head in with a frozen noodle pudding. And I'm telling you, she was worse than any of them. We just didn't think in those terms. We didn't spend our lives trying to figure out how many ways our parents screwed us up. They managed to make it through Depression and war keeping food on the table and clothes on our back, and if they didn't say "I love you" once a week or give you enough "positive reinforcement," you lived. America made too much money, that's the problem. Suddenly, we got all this time to sit around and figure out why we're still not happy. You notice it's movie stars and yuppies who go on *Donohue* and into therapy to talk about their rotten parents. Your average guy making ends meet doesn't give a rat's ass about "getting in touch with the

child within." He wants to get fed and he wants to get laid.
Done. Blaming their parents, the nerve of them. When we
were growing up, it was the kids who were the
disappointments. Is that out of fashion now, or what?
(*Pause.*) I can't say these things around Phyllis or she'll
give me the look. You know the look. The one that says,
"All right, I love you anyway." I hate that look. It doesn't
even take long for it to work, maybe half a second and I
crumble inside. Because there it is, the face of the woman
I've lived with for thirty years saying that I don't deserve
her, which I know is true, or that I don't love the kids as
much as she does, which I know she thinks, but which is
utter nonsense. I love my kids so much I want to burst.
Just look at them. They're smart, smarter than Phyllis and
me ever were. They've got a rhythm when they talk, it's
amazing, you can't keep up. They're beautiful. But, look,
I'm disappointed. Sure. Every parent has been disappointed
by their children since God with Adam and Eve. (*HE sits.*)
Suzanne, she could have been a doctor, a surgeon yet. She
had straight A's. But she likes to take the easy way out. So
she works at Bloomingdale's, a place, thank God, that
hasn't gone under. Yet. She married early, the first guy she
went with seriously. The first guy. Still, Rob's good to
her, I can't complain. And David? Oh, he could have been
... he could have been anything he wanted to be. On
television, if he wanted. With everything we did for him....
But, that's life. What are you gonna do? You give your life
for them, they disappoint you, and you love them. And
that's the gift. You find yourself able to love them, even
with all the crap. They didn't ask to come into this world.
It was our decision. You throws the dice, you takes your
chances. And you try not to think about it.

(LIGHTS up on the apartment. SUZANNE enters at the end of Walter's speech. SHE is talking on the phone.)

SUZANNE. No. I won't show for at least another month, I think. Okay, what? No way. We are not calling it David. Because you're not dead, that's why. It's spooky. I don't care what gentiles do. David ... Yeah? Okay, what if it's a girl? Davida? Davida Stein? She'd end up planting trees in the Golan Heights. You're crazy.

ROB. *(Enters the apartment with a briefcase.)* Hi.

(SHE waves to him and continues on the phone. ROB sits and goes through the day's mail.)

SUZANNE. Now, you're really pushing it. There's no way we're going to name our first born Siegfried. David, I have to go, Rob just got home. You get back to work. Make some money, we're all ashamed of you. I'm kidding. God. Okay, bye. *(SHE hangs up and kisses Rob.)*

SUZANNE. Hi. I think David is more anxious than we are.

ROB. I heard.

SUZANNE. Honey, I know this sounds ridiculous, but this afternoon, I think I felt like a kick. Not a kick, maybe, more like a knock. Like, "Hello, I'm in here." It was incredible.

ROB. That's impossible. It's too early. There's no way.

SUZANNE. What's the matter?

ROB. Sit down, we have to talk.

SUZANNE. Oh no. Oh no. Oh, God. Oh, God. It's deformed, isn't it? It has no arms or it's blind or, what? Oh, God. Oh, God. Oh, God.

ROB. (*Overlapping.*) No, no, no. No. Calm down, please, will you? It's nothing like that.

SUZANNE. Well, what?

ROB. Sit down. Let's go through it.

(ROB leads her to a chair. HE then takes out a folder from his briefcase and sits next to her. HE removes some computer printouts from the folder and lays them out in front of them.)

SUZANNE. My hands are sweating.

ROB. Okay. Dr. Lodge was very pleased with how it went. He was able to get a good sampling of the genetic material and all the tests were completed. Now remember, we're still in an experimental area. I mean, they can't guarantee that this information is 100% accurate.

SUZANNE. Will you just tell me?

ROB. Okay. It's a boy. No physical deformities.

SUZANNE. Ten fingers, ten toes?

ROB. Ten fingers, ten toes.

SUZANNE. Ten fingers and toes. Well, what then? Is it retarded?

ROB. No. As a matter of fact, it looks like it will be quite intelligent. Probably left-handed.

SUZANNE. Yeah? So ... what? What.

ROB. It will probably be like David. (*A beat.*) We matched the chromosomes from the test with the data compiled in the computer and found the presence of those genes that we've statistically linked to that trait. Then, to double check what we detected, we examined the magnetic image that we made of the brain. And, sure enough, the size of the hypothalamus is much smaller than the average, even at this early stage of development. Also, the anterior commissure connecting the cortex of the right and left sides of the brain is significantly larger than normal. Those are both in accordance with the latest studies. All of this information taken together has led Dr. Lodge to that conclusion.

SUZANNE. Oh.

ROB. He estimates it's 90% certain. But he has a big ego, so who knows? Still, the evidence suggests that that's what we've got.

(Pause.)

SUZANNE. What do we do?

ROB. I don't know.

SUZANNE. They could be wrong.

ROB. Yes. That's a definite possibility. And it's not like we can point to one gene and say "aha." It's the whole composite of evidence that's open to interpretation.

SUZANNE. So, it could be a mistake.

ROB. Adrian says 90% sure. I believe him.

SUZANNE. Can we pretend we never heard this?

ROB. Can *you*?

SUZANNE. *(Thinks a moment, then:)* No. Will any kid we have...?

ROB. That's very unlikely. There are cases of siblings, but almost never all of them.

SUZANNE. What about environment? I mean if we know before, couldn't we raise it in a way that ...

ROB. It's possible, but who knows how? And judging by how clearly it shows up in the statistical evidence, we'd have a lot of nature to nurture against. But, yes, I guess we could try something like that if you want.

SUZANNE. I tried to think of everything. All my life, I've tried to visualize bad things really clearly so they wouldn't happen, because things never happen when you expect them. But I never thought of that. I didn't know they could ...

ROB. Well, we can.

SUZANNE. Are you mad at me?

ROB. Of course not. What a stupid thing to say.

SUZANNE. But he's my brother.

ROB. It's nobody's fault. That's just the way it is.

SUZANNE. But you're upset.

ROB. I'm not thrilled.

SUZANNE. How can you be sarcastic?

ROB. I'm answering your question. Yes, I'm upset.

SUZANNE. (*Softly.*) We could get rid of it. I mean ...

(*Beat.*)

ROB. We could. Yes. We could ...

SUZANNE. (*Tentative.*) I don't *want* to ...

ROB. I know. Sure.

SUZANNE. I mean, it's not something I ever thought I'd have to do.

ROB. No. It would have to be considered very carefully.

SUZANNE. God. How ...?

ROB. We don't have to decide tonight.

SUZANNE. No, of course not.

ROB. But, you don't want to take too much time with that decision. The earlier the better.

SUZANNE. Right. I know. Oh, God. What do other people do?

ROB. What do you mean?

SUZANNE. I mean, what's the precedent?

ROB. There is no precedent. It's just us. I'm going to get out of this suit. (*HE walks to the bedroom.*)

SUZANNE. If only it were deformed.

ROB. Suzanne!

SUZANNE. It wouldn't be so complicated, that's all. This is so complicated.

ROB. We'll be okay. (*HE exits.*)

(*SUZANNE sits still for a moment. SHE then picks up the telephone and presses the speed dial button.*)

SUZANNE. (*Into phone.*) Mom? It's me. Don't get hysterical.

(*ROB appears in the hallway and looks at Suzanne. MUSIC: the "Forest Murmurs" from* Siegfried.)

End of Act I

ACT II

Scene 1

MUSIC: "The Ride of The Walküres." The LIGHTS reveal DAVID upstage center in dramatic silhouette against the sky. HE walks downstage and cuts the MUSIC off abruptly with his arms.

DAVID. Oh, sure, everybody knows that part. That's the "Ride of the Walküres." I nearly got in a fist fight with an usher who referred to it as "Theme from *Apocalypse Now*." These things are important to me. (*HE sits.*) At the end of *Götterdamerung*, Brünnhilde returns the magic ring to the river Rhine, from where it was stolen in the first place. And right after she does this, the world ends in a cataclysm of fire and water. Now, since the first performance, people have pointed out that doesn't make any sense. We're told over and over that all the trouble started when the gold was stolen from its natural place in the Rhine, so when it's put back, the curse should end and everybody should live happily ever after. The gods don't have to die, the world doesn't have to burn, we don't have to start all over. So why does it happen? Wagner went through a slew of different endings and this is the one he decided upon, he must have known what he was doing, there must be a simple explanation. And there is. When a friend asked him why it happens this way he said, "Listen to the music, you'll know." And sure enough, the arrogant little Nazi was right. You sit in the theatre and experience this onslaught of sound and destruction, and you know that it was all inevitable. This is the way everything comes to an end. I find myself in the same position when I tell friends about what happened to the Golds. They say, "I don't believe it," or "that makes no sense." And the only explanation I can give is, "If you were there, you'd know." Logic is besides the point. I think that's why I love the opera. When art is at its most outrageous, when it cannot be easily believed, that is when it most resembles life. The answers are in the experience.

(DAVID snaps his fingers. MUSIC: "The Valhalla Theme" from Das Rheingold. *The apartment slides upstage and is replaced by the kitchen of Phyllis and Walter's suburban home. A swinging door leads to the rest of the house. There's a table with two chairs right and a counter with two tall stools left. PHYLLIS stands by the counter with an urgent expression on her face.)*

DAVID. My mother called me to the house one Sunday to help her with an urgent problem.

(LIGHTS up full as DAVID joins PHYLLIS. The MUSIC fades out.)

PHYLLIS. One more time, please.
DAVID. All right. The TV and the VCR always stay on channel three.
PHYLLIS. Always?
DAVID. Always.
PHYLLIS. What if ...

DAVID. *Always*. But the cable box can go to any station you want. Now repeat what I just said.

PHYLLIS. Repeat?

DAVID. Repeat.

PHYLLIS and DAVID. The TV and the VCR *always* stay on channel three, but ...

PHYLLIS. Wait, wait, this is the hard part—but the cable box can go to any station you want. Oh, okay.

DAVID. You and Dad are really pathetic.

PHYLLIS. We're old. These things are new to us.

(SHE sits on one of the stools. DAVID hangs up his coat and then joins her on the other stool.)

DAVID. It's not that. I just find it distressing that my parents have become such a cliché.

PHYLLIS. You were always good mechanically. Hilary Klein asked you over to fix her stereo when you were fourteen. She loved you. So did her mother.

DAVID. Yes, if I remember correctly, I had my way with both of them in the garage.

PHYLLIS. Her brother's very delicate looking. You think he might be?

DAVID. I don't know, Ma. I'll check the newsletter.

PHYLLIS. Don't be such a smart-ass.

(SHE crosses to the refrigerator and pours juice for David. HE sits at the table.)

PHYLLIS. Listen, David, I want to talk to you about some things. Your father will be home soon, they usually play till three. We don't have much time.

DAVID. Mom, are you having an affair?

PHYLLIS. If I was, I wouldn't tell you.

DAVID. Ooh, listen to you.

PHYLLIS. (*Puts cookies on a plate in front of him.*) David, I want you to stop taking money from your father.

DAVID. What? What are you talking about?

PHYLLIS. I know he gives you. I'm not stupid. Besides, we talk. Children think their parents never talk to each other.

DAVID. It's not a lot.

PHYLLIS. Enough is enough. (*SHE pours a cup of coffee and sits opposite David.*)

DAVID. Mom, I'm embarking on an artistic career, it takes time before you can make enough to live decently. Especially now.

PHYLLIS. He can't afford it. Money's tight. Your father's having problems.

DAVID. Dad? What happened?

PHYLLIS. Some bad investments. Everybody's dying.

DAVID. What about at Pearson? They're indestructible, I thought.

PHYLLIS. Nobody's paying their credit card bills. People are running up their cards and not paying. They declare bankruptcy or just let the numbers skyrocket. They don't care anymore. They think, screw the system. And then there are people like you ...

DAVID. People like me?

PHYLLIS. Your age, dying. They spend like crazy and then die, they don't care.

DAVID. Good for them.

PHYLLIS. Maybe so, but it's not good for your father. Pearson goes after the families, but that takes time, and there's usually nothing there.

DAVID. God damn.

PHYLLIS. Look, your father would never admit any of this to you, so I want you to do this for me. If he offers you anything, you refuse. Find something else. All right?

DAVID. All right.

PHYLLIS. After all, you're old enough now ...

DAVID. All right.

PHYLLIS. You are spoiled, David, you know that.

DAVID. I said "all right," didn't I?

PHYLLIS. Fine. (*Rises and crosses to the sink.*)

DAVID. I've been talking to a friend at N.Y.U. about doing some teaching in the musical theatre program. I'll discuss the similarities of scenic elements in works by Verdi and Jerry Herman. I like to lecture people.

PHYLLIS. Good. Thank you, sweetheart. You're a good boy, you really are.

DAVID. What about Suzanne?

PHYLLIS. What?

DAVID. I know he gives her too. We talk. Parents think their children never talk to each other.

PHYLLIS. She'll have to cut back.

DAVID. But with the baby on the way?

(*PHYLLIS stands at the sink, her back turned.*)

DAVID. Mom, what? Is there a problem with the baby? Mom?

PHYLLIS. There's a problem.

DAVID. (*Rising.*) Oh, God, no. Did she miscarry? Nobody's told me anything.

PHYLLIS. I'm not supposed to say. Suzanne would kill me.

DAVID. It's a little late for that now.

PHYLLIS. Please, David, leave it alone.

DAVID. Mom, I'll call her right now if you don't tell me.

PHYLLIS. She may not keep it.

DAVID. Why not?

PHYLLIS. They did that test at Oxy. Rob took her in.

DAVID. And?

PHYLLIS. It's gonna be like you.

(*Pause.*)

DAVID. They can tell that?

PHYLLIS. So it seems. I had to tell you, David. That's why I called. I know how to use the cable, I'm not a moron.

DAVID. Are they sure?

PHYLLIS. They're doctors. They never say they're sure, they just tell you enough to destroy you.

DAVID. And you really think she's going to ... No, Suzanne would never even think of doing that.

PHYLLIS. Don't be so sure.

DAVID. What did she say to you?

PHYLLIS. She goes back and forth. You know your sister. As of this morning, she doesn't want it.

DAVID. (*Sitting.*) I can't believe this. Well, what can we do? Do you want me to talk to her?

PHYLLIS. Maybe, I don't know. I'm confused. I wanted your perspective. You always see things a different way, I thought it would help.

DAVID. You want me to stop her from getting rid of it?

PHYLLIS. No. Absolutely not. It's her decision. It's the woman's choice.

DAVID. Then what?

PHYLLIS. (*Sitting.*) I don't know.

DAVID. Ma, you knew I'd be upset. Why did you bring me into this?

PHYLLIS. I just ... I kept thinking of Gloria Myers. My friend.

DAVID. With the dying mother? I don't understand.

PHYLLIS. All these years, I've been telling myself we just lost touch or that we grew apart. But that wasn't it. I dropped her. I pushed her out of my life. I was afraid she'd become sick and I'd have to go through it with her. I would have to help take care of her. I didn't think I was strong enough. Or I didn't think it was worth it. She was my best friend. We went to dances together, studied for the college boards. I loved her, never had another girlfriend like her, to this day—not in this neighborhood. Yesterday, I decided to look her up. I figured, maybe it's not too late.

DAVID. And?

PHYLLIS. She moved away years ago.

DAVID. And? Did you speak to her?

PHYLLIS. She's dead. Fifteen years already. Killed herself. With pills. She was getting sick and she didn't want to be a burden to anyone.

DAVID. I'm sorry, Mom.

PHYLLIS. There were twenty years in between. Twenty years when I could have had a best friend and I didn't. Because I'm weak. Because I didn't love her enough. I have to live with that. Now I'm afraid Suzanne could make the same mistake and never know it.

DAVID. Then tell her.

PHYLLIS. I can't. I have to be supportive.

DAVID. Well, I don't.

PHYLLIS. David, please. This is her child. And Rob's.

DAVID. I don't see why this is even an issue.

PHYLLIS. That's because you're in the Arts. To other people, it's a big deal.

DAVID. Mom, I'm living it, and I don't see the problem. What difference does it make?

PHYLLIS. Come on, wouldn't you rather be ...?

DAVID. No. Maybe I did once, but not anymore. I have a happy life. I'm in a community. Are you?

PHYLLIS. David, I read the obits every week.

DAVID. And everybody's dying.

PHYLLIS. But wouldn't you rather ...?

DAVID. (*Crossing left.*) Mom, please. That's like asking wouldn't blacks rather be white?

PHYLLIS. Well, wouldn't they? David, it's common sense.

DAVID. Only because they spend their lives being shit on for what isn't their fault.

PHYLLIS. That doesn't change the reality. In this society, anyone would rather ...

DAVID. Be you.

PHYLLIS. (*Stung.*) Don't be cruel, David. You know what I'm saying.

DAVID. Fine. This is ridiculous. Look, the question is hypothetical.

PHYLLIS. Not anymore. The hypothalamus is in question. Or whatever it is. I still don't understand what they're saying.

DAVID. (*Stands behind Phyllis and puts his hands on her shoulders.*) That it's biological, it's all natural. Congratulations, Ma, you're finally off the hook.

PHYLLIS. Mmm, right. I don't buy that. It's gotta be my fault. I must have dressed you funny. Or, I don't know, if only I hadn't taken your temperature that way.

(*Pause.*)

DAVID. Mom, what would you have done? I have to know.

PHYLLIS. David, we love you.

DAVID. But if you had known.

PHYLLIS. It was a different time. Different attitudes.

DAVID. Not so different.

PHYLLIS. You were always a joy. The delivery was a breeze, you came out singing and dancing. (*Singing.*) "Matchmaker, matchmaker, make me a ..."

(*DAVID sits opposite her. Their eyes meet.*)

DAVID. Now I understand. That's why you can't talk to her yourself. Of course. Because you would have done the same thing. You would have killed me.

PHYLLIS. (*Rising.*) David, you stop that. You are my son. I raised you. I wiped your tush. I held your head over the toilet when you were sick. I gave my life for you and your sister.

DAVID. Then tell Suzanne to keep the baby.

PHYLLIS. I can't.

DAVID. You have to. Mom, don't you see what this means? For all of us.

PHYLLIS. I can't tell her anything. How can I? She's seen what I've been through with you.

DAVID. (*Stands and faces her.*) What have you been through?

PHYLLIS. I've seen my child become something ... different. That hurts, David. If you were a parent, you'd understand. This isn't what I wanted for you.

DAVID. Well, get over it!

PHYLLIS. It's not that easy. I can't.

DAVID. You could. But you don't want to. So you're letting her kill me.

PHYLLIS. No, David, no.

DAVID. You're killing me.

PHYLLIS. No, don't say that.

WALTER. (*From offstage.*) Phyllis? (*HE enters, casually dressed.*) Hey, look who's here, the Wunderkind. Hey, kiddo.

DAVID. Hi, Dad.

WALTER. (*Kisses Phyllis' cheek and pours a cup of coffee.*) I played pretty good today. Took Dennis Kaplan in straight sets. You should've heard him. Wouldn't shut up about Denise's wedding. Like I want to hear about his buck-toothed kids. Everyone knows we've got the best kids in this neighborhood. The smartest, the best looking.

DAVID. Mom told me about Suzanne.

WALTER. (*To Phyllis.*) I thought she told you not to say anything.

PHYLLIS. It wasn't right, Walter. I had to. He had to know.

WALTER. So. Look, it's their decision, David. If you get married and start a family it will be your decision. (*HE sits at the table.*) We're liberal people, maybe too much so. We let each of our children live their own lives.

DAVID. What would you have done?

WALTER. What?

PHYLLIS. He wants to know if we had known ...

WALTER. What nonsense. We didn't. We didn't know.

PHYLLIS. I told him it was a different time.

WALTER. That it was.

DAVID. I don't think the date has anything to do with it. Nothing much has changed.

WALTER. (*Crossing to the refrigerator.*) Well, maybe you're right. Phyllis, you have any of that cheese?

DAVID. Goddam it. Why is it so hard for you people to answer?

WALTER. (*Closes the refrigerator door.*) Because we don't want to. David, I gotta tell you, for a smart kid, you're pretty stupid.

PHYLLIS. Walter, please.

DAVID. Why don't you want to? What are you hiding?

WALTER. Why do you want to do this? Huh, David? What good is it gonna do?

DAVID. I think I have a right to know.

WALTER. A right? You've got some nerve. "A right." We've given you everything a kid could ask for your whole life. You have no more rights.

PHYLLIS. This is silly. Boys, you're fighting over nothing.

DAVID. No, we're not.

WALTER. You're upset because you don't know what I feel inside? Well, tough. I don't even know what I feel inside.

DAVID. (*Crosses angrily to the door and puts on his coat.*) Bullshit, Dad. You know. You just don't have the guts to tell me.

WALTER. That's it. Okay. You got it.

PHYLLIS. Walter, don't.

WALTER. No, if he wants to be so dramatic and make a scene to find out "the truth," whatever that is, then fine.

DAVID. I do.

(*FLAMES from the "Magic Fire" flicker and rise in the sky behind the scene.*)

WALTER. All right. The answer is, "Who knows?" Maybe you'd be here, maybe you wouldn't. Maybe Suzanne would be an only child. Maybe we wouldn't have to think about the things you make us think about. If you want to know what I really feel, I'll tell you. I think you're sick and diseased and if there were a cure, I'd want you cured. That's how I feel. And even though your mother may refuse to admit it, deep down, she feels the same way.

PHYLLIS. Don't you speak for me.

WALTER. Fine. Now, you can tell us till you're blue in the face that it's irrational and we're narrow-minded but it won't make any difference. That's just the way it is. Still, it doesn't change anything. You're our only son and

we love you. We love you very much, David, always have
and always will. There's your answer.

(The FLAMES disappear. A short pause.)

DAVID. Thank you. I appreciate your honesty. It's
refreshing.

PHYLLIS. Don't listen to him, David. He doesn't
mean it.

WALTER. Will you stop it, Phyllis. He can handle it.
He's a man now. He's tough.

DAVID. Getting tougher by the minute.

WALTER. Good. Atta boy. That's right. You look
good. Doesn't he look good? So, when are you going to
come play tennis with me?

DAVID. Dad, you're a demon on the court. I wouldn't
have a chance.

WALTER. Aah. Hey, mister, you need any money to
tide you over? (*HE takes money out of his wallet and offers
it.*)

DAVID. No, that's okay.

PHYLLIS. Don't spoil him, Walter.

WALTER. What spoil, he works hard. Here. Take,
take.

DAVID. No, that's all right, Dad. I don't need it. I'm
starting to do some teaching on the side at N.Y.U. Next
week. It pays well.

WALTER. That's terrific.

DAVID. Yeah. I have to go.

PHYLLIS. David, you want any food to take home?

DAVID. No. Thanks, Mom. (*HE takes a long look at
both of them.*) Thanks. Bye. (*HE exits. A slight pause.*)

WALTER. That's good about N.Y.U.
PHYLLIS. Mmm. Yeah. (*SHE looks at him.*)
WALTER. Don't look.

(*HE exits right. PHYLLIS is left alone. SHE takes a
moment to regain her composure.*)

Scene 2

PHYLLIS addresses the audience.

PHYLLIS. We live in the Information Age. It's true.
Every Sunday, while Walter plays tennis, I sit in bed with
all *The New York Times* from the week, Monday to
Sunday. (*SHE sits at the kitchen table.*) The kids make fun
of me. They say, "Mom, read 'The Week In Review,'
that's all you need. You're gonna be out of date anyway."
Still, I lie there reading everything I didn't get to. It's a
compulsion, a disease. I'm so afraid I'll be caught in
conversation without knowing what Anthony Lewis wrote
about Israel on Tuesday and I'll be sent to Jewish Liberal
detention. I get very nervous. Anyway, it takes me the
whole day and I usually finish the week's pile just in time
for *60 Minutes* which we watch to see if Mike Wallace is
destroying anyone we know. That's how I start the week.
My brain is so full of news and issues, opinions and
statistics, that sometimes I have to read Danielle Steele
just to clear my head. Otherwise, I wake up screaming,
"I'll take social injustice for six hundred, Alex!" (*SHE rises
and clears the table.*) You always hear people say we don't

know enough. We're all ignorant, that's why the country's falling apart. Well, I don't see that, not for a minute. If you ask me, I think we all know too damn much. We're all being oppressed by information that has nothing to do with our experience. All we can do is react. Years ago, we didn't know about blacks. Not really. They were blacks, live and let live. We didn't know about sex, how it was supposed to feel, what to do. Who thought it was supposed to be any better than it was? (*SHE steps off the kitchen set and crosses downstage center.*) We didn't know about addictions, about life in prison, about the plight of transexual, cross-dressing, priests. Right? Years ago, you lived your life. Now, we have to seem so concerned all the time about every terrible, unfair thing that goes on, that we all walk around with these pained Barbara Walters expressions plastered on our faces. And what good is it doing? Not only have we completely failed at helping anybody else, but we have taken the beauty and simplicity out of our own lives. Am I right? (*Pause.*) This is a terrible thing I'm saying. I know. It sounds like I'm advocating ignorance, wanting to look the other way. But I'm not. I think people are good and should be left alone. If they could just do what their hearts tell them to do, everything would be all right. If they would just listen to their hearts. Sometimes, I hear people around here say, "If my daughter did this," or "If my son was like that, I'd run him out of the house." And I want to say, "No, you wouldn't. That's very easy for you to say, sitting there with your Vuitton bag, driving your Infiniti, and expecting the world to cater to you. But you don't know how you'd feel. You don't know how your heart breaks when the world around you doesn't match your expectations. You have no idea." That's what I want to tell them. But it's none of their business. So I don't say anything. I just sit there. I don't say anything.

(MUSIC: The "Fate Motive" from Die Walküre. The kitchen moves offstage as the LIGHTS come up on Suzanne and Rob's apartment. There is a KNOCK at the door. SUZANNE enters nervously from the kitchen. SHE looks at the door, not knowing what to do. The KNOCKING continues. Finally, SHE speaks.)

SUZANNE. Yes?

DAVID. (Through the door.) Open up, you rich bitch.

SUZANNE. David, you shit.

DAVID. (Opens the door with his key.) I'm gonna smash your Krups cappuccino maker.

SUZANNE. Very funny.

DAVID. Hi, sis. I called Bloomingdale's, they said you left early, so I thought I'd catch you, see how you're doing.

SUZANNE. I had a headache.

DAVID. That reminds me, this is for you. (HE takes out a CD from his pocket.)

SUZANNE. Gypsy. Well, at least it's not opera.

DAVID. This is the Angela Lansbury recording. I already gave you the original with Merman, but I saw last time I was here that you still haven't opened it. So I figure two different versions improves my chances.

SUZANNE. You're really starting to piss me off.

DAVID. Please, if I wanted to piss you off, I'd bring Tyne Daly.

SUZANNE. Put it with the others. I know how you like them in alphabetical order.

DAVID. My pleasure.

SUZANNE. I'm making dinner. There's not enough food, you can't stay.

(SHE exits to the kitchen. DAVID looks at the CD collection. HE picks up a boxed opera set.)

DAVID. I don't believe it! It can't be! "Vittoria"!

SUZANNE. What are you yelling about?

DAVID. The *La Bohème* is out of the plastic. There's hope!

SUZANNE. *(From the kitchen.)* Don't get excited. *Moonstruck* was on cable.

DAVID. From me it's boring ...

SUZANNE. Honestly, David, I wish you'd stop bringing us that stuff. It puts me in a very awkward position.

DAVID. I don't take it personally. Besides, it's not for you anymore.

SUZANNE. Rob has no interest.

DAVID. Somebody will.

(Pause. SUZANNE enters.)

SUZANNE. Mom told you. I knew she would. This family talks too much.

DAVID. So then it's true. How can you? Do you realize what you're doing?

SUZANNE. Funny, I don't remember asking for your input.

DAVID. Suzanne, I can't just sit by and let this happen.

SUZANNE. Stop it, David. Stop it before you say another word. You have no right to come in here and tell me what to do. Especially after Marnie Eisner.

DAVID. What? Marnie Eisner? I can't believe you're throwing that in my face.

SUZANNE. You were a junior in high school. You came to me in a panic, your voice was cracking. You said, "Suzanne, I don't know what to do. I can't have a kid. I won't be able to go to college." Remember?

DAVID. It just happened.

SUZANNE. Do you remember how I went with you to the bank and we got out some of your Bar Mitzvah money? Do you?

DAVID. Of course I do. I remember.

SUZANNE. I brought the two of you to that clinic that smelled like Windex. I held her hand. I held your hand. I took care of both of you and we got it done.

DAVID. Yes, you were wonderful.

SUZANNE. You were so afraid Mom and Dad would find out.

DAVID. Now it's what they pray for.

SUZANNE. Whatever happened to Marnie?

DAVID. She lives with a woman in Seattle. I think we both knew something wasn't right. So, what's your point?

SUZANNE. I supported you. No questions asked. Now I want you to do the same thing.

DAVID. I'm sorry, I can't do that.

SUZANNE. David!

DAVID. It's not the same thing. Not even remotely. Marnie got pregnant by accident. Her life would have been badly damaged, as would mine, and so would the kid's. You and Rob wanted this baby. You can afford it. You're ready to be parents. But now, because you know something about this person you've created that you don't care for, you're ending his life.

SUZANNE. It's my choice, David. It's my right to choose. And stop saying "his."

DAVID. Ah, yes, the right of choice—the last refuge of the morally indefensible. We demand the right of choice when we know deep down what we want to do is wrong. Necessary maybe, regrettable yes, but definitely wrong. We demand our God-given right to take the easy way out.

SUZANNE. You don't believe that.

DAVID. Yes. Right now, I think I do.

SUZANNE. No, I know you don't. You're talking like some Right-Wing Fundamentalist crackpot. Coming here in your own little "Operation Rescue." Don't you dare give me a sermon as if you had morality on your side. I think we know you don't.

DAVID. That's not what this is about. I would never take away your right. I'd march in the streets and write my congressman to make sure you keep it. But this is something new. This is a decision that no one's ever had to make before. I'm asking you to choose carefully. Please. Think it over.

SUZANNE. I have.

DAVID. Think harder. How can you do this to me?

SUZANNE. Oh, this is about you, is it?

DAVID. You're erasing me from the world. You're rubbing me out. Why? I thought you loved me.

SUZANNE. Don't play those games with me. They won't work.

(Beat.)

DAVID. What does Rob say?

SUZANNE. Rob says a lot. He says he'll be patient and support me in my choice but I should hurry up and decide. And if I feel up to the challenge of raising this one then he is too. The message is coming through loud and clear: Why put ourselves through this? And, frankly, I don't blame him. This baby was going to change our lives and make everything better. Not that things are bad, but, I don't know, we could use a clear sense of purpose. Now the whole thing is tainted. I wish we didn't know, but we do. And it's a problem.

DAVID. What wouldn't be a problem with you?

SUZANNE. Oh, please.

DAVID. What if you found out the kid was going to be ugly, or smell bad, or have an annoying laugh, or need really thick glasses?

SUZANNE. Come on, David. We're talking about something pretty serious.

DAVID. But where do we stop? You know we have relatives who died for less. So now we have this technology, what are we going to do with it? It starts with us, Suzanne.

SUZANNE. Oh, shut up! Shut up! Shut up! I can't take it anymore.

DAVID. That's because you know I'm right.

SUZANNE. No, it's because I'm sick of you. I'm tired of your lectures and the way you talk down to all of us. Goddam it, I am so sick of being "the shallow one." Everybody dotes on you, with all your deep feelings and higher interests. The truth is you're just a spoiled brat who always has to have his own way.

DAVID. (*Putting on his coat, crossing to the door.*)
Yes. You're right. And so is Stephen. I'm a horrible little
shit. I should get the hell out and grow up. And maybe I
will. But when I'm done, I'll come back and say the same
things and I'll still be right. (*HE opens the door.*)

SUZANNE. (*Faltering.*) Why are you doing this?

DAVID. (*Stops in the doorway.*) Because I'm fighting
for my life. Do you have any idea how horrifying this is?
To find out that the people who brought you into this
world wish that they had slammed the door?

SUZANNE. This family has been very good to you in
every way, David. Don't play the martyr. We all love you,
you know that. We love you.

DAVID. Then love him.

SUZANNE. (*With a pained sigh.*) I don't have the
strength for it. I wish to God I was as strong as you are,
but I'm not. I can't take it.

DAVID. Is that a good enough reason?

SUZANNE. (*Sitting.*) Probably not. But, think of that
little boy. What would it be like for him? You know how
people are. How would Rob and I be able to help him,
feeling the way we do? It wouldn't be fair to any of us.
David, what kind of mother would I be if I didn't
understand my child?

DAVID. I'd say you'd be pretty typical.

SUZANNE. I doubt that. This isn't typical. You're not
typical. There's nothing typical about you. You're still a
mystery to me.

DAVID. Just like you are to me. But I consider that an
asset. (*HE kneels beside her.*)

SUZANNE. David, I know it's been hard for you. When I think of all the times I've heard you say you're lonely or scared ...

DAVID. You never feel that way?

SUZANNE. You tell me your problems and it terrifies me.

DAVID. Don't make me regret sharing my life with you.

SUZANNE. Why should we put someone else through that if we can help it? Why isn't it more humane to wait until we can bring a child with no disadvantages into the world?

DAVID. Because we'll lose too much. Don't you see? All the things you love about me are tied to that one element that makes you queasy. Every human being is a tapestry. You pull one thread, one undesirable color, and the art unravels. You end up staring at the walls. When Brünnhilde dies ...

SUZANNE. (*Rising, crossing to the door.*) Oh, God, here we go. I should have known this was coming.

DAVID. When she throws herself into the fire and lets the gods die with her, she is hoping something better will rise out of the ashes. She doesn't stick around to choose what that something is. She leaves that to Nature and Fate. Hers is an act of love. That's our only hope.

SUZANNE. (*Opening the door for him.*) That's beautiful. I can skip Course in Miracles this week. Are you finished?

DAVID. (*Crosses slowly to the door and closes it.*) One more story and then I'll go. You can battle it out with your own conscience when I'm gone. But I won't leave here until you hear about Siegmund and Sieglinde.

SUZANNE. (*Sighs. SHE sits on the sofa and glances at her watch.*) Go ahead.

DAVID. Siegmund and Sieglinde are brother and sister, twins, separated in childhood. Years later, they meet and they fall in love.

SUZANNE. This is gross.

DAVID. (*Bursting with frustrated anger.*) For once, will you open your ears and really listen?! This is the only way I can make sense of things.

SUZANNE. (*Quietly.*) Sorry.

DAVID. They fall in love. And then they realize who they are. But this knowledge only spurs them on further, and in a fit of ecstasy, they consummate their feelings for each other.

SUZANNE. I don't know where you're going with this, but I think I better tell you, it's out of the question.

DAVID. (*Sits next to her.*) Siegmund is killed for his crime against the laws of morality. And Sieglinde, facing a life without her beloved brother, seeks only death. But before she ends her life, Brünnhilde tells her that she cannot die. For she is carrying Siegmund's child. She is bringing her brother's child into the world. Sieglinde is overjoyed. She hides in the forest and gives her life in the delivery of a new incarnation of her brother.

SUZANNE. What happens to her son?

(*MUSIC: the "Siegfried Idyll" played softly in the background.*)

DAVID. He is Siegfried, the bravest hero the world has ever known. Without fear, he breaks all of the gods' outdated laws in two. He follows his heart and what he learns from Nature. He understands the calls of birds. He's beautiful.

(The sky has turned clear and radiant.)

SUZANNE. And what does he do?
DAVID. He slays a dragon and walks through rings of Magic Fire. He then awakens Brünnhilde from her sleep. She tells him that she is the feminine side of himself and the two proclaim their love. By joining with her, Siegfried reaches man's true potential, both masculine and feminine, brave and loving.
SUZANNE. What happens to Siegfried?

(Gradually, the sky grows dark and cloudy and the MUSIC fades out.)

DAVID. The world, which is cruel and corrupt, destroys him. He is stabbed in the back by evil men. Such a hero cannot survive in a decaying civilization.
SUZANNE. So Sieglinde went through all that pain for nothing.
DAVID. She brought a beautiful hero into the world.
SUZANNE. And the world destroyed him. I don't want that to happen to my child.
DAVID. Then change the world.
SUZANNE. David, look at me. I couldn't finish pre-med, you want me to change the world.
DAVID. You can do this.
SUZANNE. David, you know I don't like to be tested. I just want the life Mom and Dad had when we were kids. I

want to live in the world we saw growing up. That's all I ask.

DAVID. We can't have that. Even if it existed in the first place, which I doubt, it's out of our grasp now. We don't have what our parents had. We don't have the faith, we don't have the money. We don't have the leaders, the confidence, or trust. And so, what do we do to combat the malaise? We shut ourselves off. We shrink from any challenge and take the easy way out. We've become lazy and fearful because we doubt our ability to love. Without question. I know you, Suzanne. You have the strength. You can do this. You're not shallow.

SUZANNE. You don't think so?

DAVID. No. That's a card you play because it's easy. But that's not you. I know you. There's greatness in you, Suzanne Gold. Don't be afraid. Awaken. Usher in a new era, take care of your child. Okay? Okay?

SUZANNE. (*After a moment.*) You know what I was just thinking about?

DAVID. No, what?

SUZANNE. Your bar mitzvah.

DAVID. Really?

SUZANNE. You wore that brown three-piece suit with Pierre Cardin's name written like fifty times on the back of the vest. And a really thick tie.

DAVID. You were wearing culottes.

SUZANNE. They were gauchos. But who's counting? I was so proud of you. I remember when you finished your Haftorah and you looked up, you looked right at me.

DAVID. You gave me one of these. (*HE wipes his brow and makes a "whew" sound.*)

SUZANNE. I remember thinking, how incredible. I look in his face and I see my own.

DAVID. At the party, I danced the first slow dance with you.

SUZANNE. What was the song? It was some Top 40 ballad.

DAVID. It was Roberta Flack.

SUZANNE. Oh, God, you're right.

DAVID. (*Quietly sings the song, "Killing Me Softly."*) "I heard he sang a good song, I heard he had a style ..."

(DAVID rises. HE takes Suzanne's hand and leads her to the center of the room. SHE joins him in a very slow, almost motionless dance.)

SUZANNE. Oh, God.

DAVID. (*Singing.*) "And so I came to see him to listen for a while."

SUZANNE. (*Singing.*) "And there he was this young boy, a stranger to my eyes."

BOTH. (*Singing softly and dancing.*) "Strumming my pain with his fingers, singing my life with his words..."

(The song trails off. DAVID hugs her.)

DAVID. Don't. Please don't. Don't do it. Don't.

(MUSIC: The "Love Gaze" from Act I of Die Walküre. *ROB has appeared downstage left to watch his wife and brother-in-law dance. The LIGHTS fade and DAVID and SUZANNE exit.)*

Scene 3

ROB examines the DNA model. HE turns and addresses the audience.

ROB. My favorite toy as a kid was always Lego. I must have had more Lego blocks by the time I was ten than that city in Denmark where they have that whole Lego metropolis. I could never understand the attraction of a toy that came ready in the package. What good was that? I would beg my parents to only buy me toys that said "Assembly Required." And then I would see how fast I could put the stuff together without ever reading the instructions. It didn't always come out looking like the picture on the box, but it was more important for me to attain that feeling of fulfillment. The power of the creator. I know it sounds ridiculous, but I think my road to a career in genetic research was paved with Lego. I always had a fascination with components; how things are put together, how to take them apart, how to change them. (*HE sits.*) It still excites me. I sit there in the lab, surrounded by these million dollar machines under those buzzing fluorescent lights and I think, why not with people? There's obviously a lot, we can all agree, that needs to be corrected. Or can at least be improved. Just look at the amount of suffering, inward and outward, all around us. Let's use every weapon we have to combat it. Is that such a horrible thing to think? Of course not. Well, my father turned bright red when I said something similar at the dinner table. He called me a Nazi. "You are hateful," he said. "Why has God punished us with a Nazi for a son?" So then I called him a backward little man living in the Stone Age. At which point, my mother started crying and running around lighting candles. Things haven't been the same since. (*Beat.*) I had pretty much put that whole argument out of my mind until David started his crusade. It's a complicated issue, of course it is. I don't deny that. But I can make a helluva case that what Oxy does is a lot more useful and productive for society than spending tax dollars to have fat Germans walk around a stage with helmets and spears for five hours. How dare he raise the specter of genocide, like some college kid saying anything to win an argument! The nerve of him. Suzanne and I have enough problems without him poking around her conscience. Or mine. Let's face it, do I want a kid who's going to know every time he looks in Suzanne's eyes that he's not the one she wanted? I know what that's like. My wife is not someone who has learned to live with disappointment. And I have much too well. Someone has to tell her that. (*Pause.*) The bottom line is this: Look around you. You think it's so easy to have a family today? The family is an endangered species. There are kids on the streets, broken homes, abuse. Why stack the deck against us? Why walk into a no-win situation? Don't believe what David says. This isn't an opera about the fate of humanity.

(*WALTER and PHYLLIS enter quietly through the front door. WALTER puts down their coats and the TWO sit together on the sofa.*)

ROB. It's the simple story of one family making a very private decision. He, of all people, should know to respect other people's privacy. We need to do what's right for us. Don't put the fate of the world on our shoulders. We can't carry the load.

(*LIGHTS up in the apartment. The sky is bleak and colorless.*)

PHYLLIS. Is she all right?
ROB. She's still weak. But she's glad to be home.
PHYLLIS. Should I go in?
ROB. Just leave her alone. She'll be okay.
WALTER. Let her rest.

(*Pause.*)

PHYLLIS. So what did he say, Doctor, what is it, Hagen? [*pronounced "Hay-gen"*]
WALTER. Phyllis.
PHYLLIS. I want to hear it. We hardly hear from you in weeks, you cancel dinner, and now this. I want to know what happened. What did he say?
ROB. Nothing. That there were complications.
PHYLLIS. Tell me.
WALTER. What good will it do?
PHYLLIS. I want to know.
ROB. There's always a danger when it's done after the fifth month. Dr. Hagen said there was a perforation during the procedure and Suzanne started hemorrhaging.
PHYLLIS. She always bled badly as a little girl. Like me with a paper cut.
ROB. It's genetic. Things got bad. He had to perform a hysterectomy.

PHYLLIS. Oh, God.

WALTER. Is there anything we can ...?

ROB. Nothing. She never will.

PHYLLIS. It's like a bad dream. Huh, Walter? It's a nightmare. When does it end? How many times do you have to have your heart broken? Huh, Walter?

WALTER. I know. I know.

(Pause.)

PHYLLIS. How are you doing, Rob?

ROB. I'm all right.

PHYLLIS. Have you spoken to your parents?

ROB. No. Are you kidding?

PHYLLIS. Did David call?

ROB. I spoke to him last night. He hasn't called today.

WALTER. That's surprising.

PHYLLIS. He should be here.

ROB. Why? He's done enough damage.

WALTER. What's that supposed to mean?

ROB. It's his fault. Christ, she was all set, she had made up her mind. We agreed. And then he had to interfere. He made us think too much.

PHYLLIS. You can understand how he felt. It's a very personal issue to him.

ROB. It was none of his business. You shouldn't have told him.

WALTER. Maybe not.

PHYLLIS. He's family. I had to tell him. I had to. I thought he would add a different perspective.

ROB. *(Rises, crosses upstage.)* We didn't need it. God, what is wrong with you people? Don't you have lives of your own? When are you going to leave your children alone? Stop calling, stop taking us to dinner and choosing the restaurant. Once, just once, I want to go where *I* want to go. All this closeness is suffocating.

WALTER. Fine, you want us to leave you alone, fine.

PHYLLIS. Rob, you're upset, it's understandable. Something terrible has happened.

ROB. It's more than that. You know the first thing Suzanne said to me when it was over? "Did you call my parents?" We had just lost any hope of having children and she's running to you to make her feel better. I don't know why I'm even here.

PHYLLIS. What are you saying? You're walking out? Is that what you're saying? Your wife needs you.

ROB. No, she needs you.

PHYLLIS. (*Rising.*) Don't you dare, Rob. Don't you dare.

WALTER. If he wants to go, let him go. She'll be all right. We can take care of her.

ROB. I know you can. You always do.

PHYLLIS. Walter, stop. Don't talk like that. I can't stand it.

WALTER. (*Standing, crossing right.*) It's typical of their generation. They expect too much and then they cry bloody murder when things don't work out the way they want.

PHYLLIS. I'm dying from all this. I'm dying.

(*SUZANNE appears upstage wearing a bathrobe.*)

WALTER. What are you doing up?

ROB. (*Goes to Suzanne.*) Are you okay? Take it easy. I'm here. I'm not going anywhere.

SUZANNE. I want to sit for a while.

ROB. (*Guides her slowly to the reading chair.*) Careful.

(*SUZANNE sits. ROB stands by her.*)

SUZANNE. I figure you're all talking about me anyway.

PHYLLIS. It will be all right, sweetheart.

SUZANNE. No it won't.

WALTER. Hey. Don't worry, Suzy-Q. It's not the end of the world.

SUZANNE. (*Dryly.*) Oh, that's good.

PHYLLIS. Sweetheart, tell us what happened.

WALTER. Phyllis, she doesn't feel well.

SUZANNE. No, it's all right. Might as well get it over with. What do you want to know?

PHYLLIS. When did you change your mind?

ROB. Which time?

WALTER. What the hell is wrong with you?

(*PHYLLIS steps between Walter and Rob. WALTER turns away. PHYLLIS sits.*)

SUZANNE. It's okay, Dad, leave him alone. I was just about ready to have it done. I was. I was fine with it. But then David made his case. Oh, he's good. He should have been a lawyer. He made me feel like this Anita Bryant Nazi snuffing out my own brother in cold blood.

PHYLLIS. Well, he shouldn't have done that. That wasn't right.

SUZANNE. No, it wasn't. It was very easy for him. David could make his argument, make me cry and leave. He wouldn't have to raise it. We would. The whole thing had a lot more to do with Rob and me than it did with David.

WALTER. But you listened to him.

SUZANNE. I couldn't help it. You know how he gets. I love David. I couldn't do that to him. So, I decided that I would handle it.

ROB. We talked it over.

SUZANNE. Rob was really good about it.

WALTER. Very nice. (*HE sits.*)

PHYLLIS. You told me. I was happy. So, then what?

SUZANNE. Then I started to show. Every morning, I would see it in the mirror and I'd start thinking these awful things. Mean, stupid things. I knew they were stupid. But I can't help what I think, can I? A person has no control over their feelings, right? That's what I told myself.

ROB. She was wavering, I could tell. She kept wearing big sweaters so people wouldn't notice. So she didn't have to talk about it.

SUZANNE. I got really upset, like maybe this was just too much for me.

PHYLLIS. Suzanne, why didn't you come to me?

SUZANNE. Why? Because you would have told David, that's why.

PHYLLIS. No, I wouldn't. Not if you told me not to …

SUZANNE. (*Turns away.*) About a month ago, Rob asked Dr. Lodge to recommend a counselor, someone to help us prepare for what we were facing.

ROB. Which was tricky because nobody's supposed to know about this. But Adrian found us someone he trusted.

WALTER. You were going to a counselor?

PHYLLIS. I couldn't talk about that type of thing with anyone.

SUZANNE. What a coincidence. Neither could I. We were in the cab on the way to our first appointment and I started freaking out.

ROB. I'd never seen her get like that. She started hyperventilating and wringing her hands.

SUZANNE. It was like the S.A.T.'s. I couldn't go through with it. I just couldn't. I wasn't prepared. I had to get it out.

WALTER. So you should have done it. Right then. Right away.

SUZANNE. We tried.

ROB. It took us over three weeks to find somebody willing to do it that late without asking why. Remember we couldn't tell anybody the reason.

SUZANNE. So much for freedom of choice.

ROB. Dr. Lodge refused to help. Didn't want the responsibility, he said. We found Hagen, we thought, just in time.

WALTER. That witch doctor. I should kill him.

SUZANNE. It's funny. I knew there was a risk of things going wrong, so I was sure it wouldn't happen because things never happen when you expect them. Wrong again. And now it's all over.

ROB. Stop it, Suzanne. It's not your fault.

SUZANNE. Then whose is it?

PHYLLIS. It's mine. I should have known. I should have stopped you.

SUZANNE. Mom, would you please not co-opt my failure? I'd like to have my own trauma for a change. We can cut the "sins of the mother" routine, I'm tired of it. I did this. It was time for me to take responsibility for my life. (*Laughing sadly to herself.*) Look how good I did.

(*The PHONE rings. ROB answers.*)

ROB. Hello? Oh, hi. (*To the others.*) It's Stephen.
WALTER. What's he doing, calling here?
PHYLLIS. Where's David? He should be here. Tell him I want to see him. (*Rising, calling into the phone.*) David, you should be here!
ROB. (*Into phone.*) She's doing okay. I brought her home this morning. Yeah. What? Uh-huh. (*HE goes to the CD collection.*) Okay, I see it. Yeah. Okay, bye.
WALTER. Is David coming?
ROB. No. He asked Stephen to call, to make sure Suzanne was all right. He told me to look for a note.
WALTER. What?

(*ROB pulls a note out of the boxed* Ring *cycle.*)

PHYLLIS. How did he get it here?
SUZANNE. David has a key.
PHYLLIS. But why would he stick it in there?
SUZANNE. It's a place we'd never look.

(*ROB unfolds the note and finds David's keys to the apartment. HE hands them to SUZANNE. HE sits on the floor next to her.*)

WALTER. What's it say? Read it.

ROB. "To the last of the Golds: I want to express my deepest sympathy for what has happened. And so does Stephen. This is a difficult time, I know, and I am sorry that I am not there with you, but I'm afraid I can never see any of you again. I never ..."

WALTER. What?

SUZANNE. Let him finish.

(The sky turns red.)

ROB. "I never dreamed I would or could leave you all, but now I know that I have no choice. You are creating a new world for yourselves and it is one of which I will never be a part. Please, however, don't pity me, for I am not alone."

WALTER. He's so dramatic.

PHYLLIS. Oh my God.

(The sky returns slowly to a peaceful blue.)

ROB. "I know you love me. And I love you all so much. But we are weak people. You don't love me enough to allow me into your family, and I don't love you enough not to notice. Don't try to contact me, I won't respond. This is the dawn of a new era. *Ruhe, ruhe, du Gott.* Love, David."

(Pause.)

PHYLLIS. Do something, Walter, call him.

WALTER. He told us not to.

PHYLLIS. Suzanne, he'll listen to you. Call him. Say you're sorry.

SUZANNE. No. He's right.

PHYLLIS. What?

SUZANNE. He's right.

PHYLLIS. What are you saying?

WALTER. It's what he wants.

PHYLLIS. Oh, God. Oh, my God.

WALTER. Let him go, Phyllis. Just let him go.

PHYLLIS. No! I won't let him go. He's our son. I can't let him go! We're not the people who cut off their children. We're not the people who do that. Walter, please!

WALTER. Shh. Phyllis, shh.

ROB. Sit down, Mom.

SUZANNE. (*Flatly, remembering David's story.*) "Rest. Rest."

(*Pause. There is a KNOCK at the door. The LIGHTS fade as the apartment walls return and re-form the apartment as it appeared in the opening moments of the play. MUSIC: Prelude to* Siegfried, *Act Two.*
DAVID *enters downstage right. The MUSIC fades out.*)

DAVID. A few weeks later, Stephen and I celebrated our third anniversary. To prove to him how much I had matured in my new sense of independence and manhood, I let him arrange the evening. He took me to a Bruce Springsteen concert. And people say *Tristan* is long! But I liked it. I'm used to hearing people sing for four hours without understanding a word. Afterwards, we went home and gave each other gifts. We're not crazy about crystal and glass, so we checked out what the third anniversary is according to tradition. Anyone know? Leather. That we liked. (*HE smiles.*) Relax. He gave me a wallet. (*HE looks at the FAMILY, still in tableau.*) I've been true to my word. To this day, I haven't spoken to the Golds. It hasn't been easy. More than once my mother showed up at our apartment in the middle of the night, crying and pounding on the door. But I just buried my head in Stephen's chest until my father came and dragged her away. Dad didn't share Mom's flair for melodrama. He just sent me checks, which he knew I wouldn't cash, accompanied by notes that read, "How can you do this to your mother?" I never heard from Suzanne. She understood. But maybe they all do now. I never hear from anyone anymore. (*Beat.*) Once, just once, I almost broke down and called the Golds. A conductor friend of mine invited Stephen and me over for dinner to introduce us to his very distinguished new boyfriend. None other than Dr. Adrian Lodge. "Jewish anti-semites, they're the worst." Right, Ma? (*HE smiles.*) I hardly ever listen to *The Ring Cycle* now. Still, I talk about it in my course at N.Y.U. I'm famous for my lecture about the Magic Fire, not because it's so insightful, but because I usually break down and cry. (*HE lectures.*) So, what is the Magic Fire? Shaw wrote, it is the Lie that must hide the Truth. It's the teachings of the Church, the laws of the State. It's the fire of Hell that will burn you if you question what you're told. It's everything you're afraid of because you're supposed to be. But then how come Siegfried walks right through it without so much as singeing an eyebrow? It's not because he's such a hero. Most of the time he's played by a tenor who looks like Ed Asner in a blonde wig. It's because the Magic Fire is a fraud.

(MUSIC: The statement of the "Love and Redemption" theme that ends The Ring.*)*

DAVID. It can't hurt you. Mankind will keep creating new and better worlds, and there will always be those who are left, for whatever reason, on the other side of the Magic Fire. If only we were brave enough to walk through that fire, and unlock that door, we would awaken another part of our soul. And we would know what it means to truly love. Without question. *(The MUSIC swells.)* Just listen to that.

(The glorious final chord hovers, suspended over David as HE takes a seat downstage and looks at the GOLDS, still in tableau. The last thread of sound dies away as the LIGHTS slowly fade to BLACK.)

Curtain

End of Play

COSTUME PLOT

DAVID

I-1
2 chambray shirts
Multi-print tie
Taupe pants
Brown belt
Brown shoes, thick
Brown Topsiders
2 pairs taupe socks
Gray wool blazer
Overcoat w/red ribbon
Brown leather bag
Brown watch
Scarf

II-1
Black jeans
Long johns shirt
Plaid flannel shirt
Black Dr. Marten shoes
2 pairs thick black socks
Black belt

II-2
Same black jeans
2 black t-shirts
Green sweater
Black belt
Black socks
Black shoes
Bomber jacket

Final Monologue
Same as I-1

WALTER

I-1
Navy double-breasted suit
White French-cuff shirt
Tie
Black dress shoes
2 pairs black dress socks
Black belt
Gold tennis racket tie clip
Dark grey overcoat
Gold watch
3 white hankies
I-2 Monologue
Same as above, lose jacket
II-2
Gray flannel pants
Burgundy polo shirt
Members Only jacket
2 pairs white sweat socks
White Reebok tennis shoes
Brown alligator wallet
Black belt
II-3
Taupe pants
Tan button-down shirt
Black belt
Black shoes
Black socks
Dark grey overcoat

ROB
I-1&2
Black & white sweater
Blue button-down shirt
Burgundy print tie
Black suspenders
Black dress shoes
2 pairs black thick socks
Black cashmere overcoat
Gold watch
I-3
Gray suit
White button-down shirt
Burgundy-tan tie
Black belt
Black shoes
Black socks
Black overcoat
Burgundy suspenders
II-3
Chino pants
Blue sweatshirt, pullover
2 pairs white athletic socks
White Nike tennis shoes
Brown leather belt
Wallet

PHYLLIS
I-1
Cream shit
Cream heels
6 pairs nylon hose

Cream beaded clutch
Pearl & silver earrings
Fur coat
II-1
Denim shirt
Dark blue pants
Black belt
Black shoes, low heeled
Gold earrings
Hose
II-3
Dark taupe suit
Black heels, higher heels
Gold knot earrings
Gold mesh necklace
Fur coat
Pantyhose
Gold round pin
Lavender slippers

SUZANNE
I-1&2
Black beaded sweater
Black silk skirt
Black heels
Black pantyhose
Diamond stud earrings
Gold/diamond wedding ring set
Double strand black jet beads
Black overcoat
Tan apron
Black bra

Hair accessories
I-3
Burgundy/white dress
White sweater
2 pairs white crew socks
Single strand pearls
Pearl studs
II-2
Chinos
White shirt
2 pairs white crew socks
White Converse sneakers
Single strand pearl necklace
Pearl earrings
Brown belt
II-3
Peach robe
Cream nightshirt
Slippers

PROPERTY LIST

City skyline
Fortunoff bag with *The Ring* CD in yellow Tower Records
  bag
Crystal-handled cheese slicer
Gift box tied with ribbon
Crystal clock
David's keys
Rob's keys
Rob's mail
Briefcase with manilla folder with three pieces of computer
  printout paper
David's satchel
David's coat
Walter's coat
Phyllis' coat & purse
La Bohème CD
Sofa (two pillows, one at each end)
Sofa table
5 coasters
Lamp
Ashtray
Napkins
Club chairs
Hassock
Tray
Stereo
DNA model
12 disc cases
Swivel chair
Scientific journals

Ottoman
Notebook
Butcher block
4 wine glasses
3 water glasses
2 highball glasses
Dishrag
Bottle of Evian
Scotch bottle
Bottle opener
Tiffany gift box
Ice in bucket
Cutting board
Paring knife
Limes
Sponge
Ring in small box
Phone
Rob & Suzanne's coats
Gym bag
Plate w/ carrots & celery
Bowl of dip
Plate w/low-fat cheese & knife
Bowl of crackers
Bow of peanuts
Wine bottle in bucket
Kitchen towel
Gypsy CD
Refrigerator
Juice
Cookies in cookie jar
Coffee pot with coffee (Decaf)

Towels
Tissues
Juice Glass
Coffee cups
Television
2 bar stools
David's satchel
Kitchen table with 2 chairs
Step stool

Perishables

Fat-free cheddar cheese
Celery & carrots (cut in very thin strips)
Low-fat sour cream
Lipton Onion Soup mix
Wheat Thins
Bottle water
Decaf coffee
White grape juice
Dry-roasted peanuts
Chips Ahoy
Throat drops
Tissues
Water cups
Dishwashing liquid
Cocktail napkins
Wrapping paper
Apple juice
Limes (to be sliced on stage)
Lemons

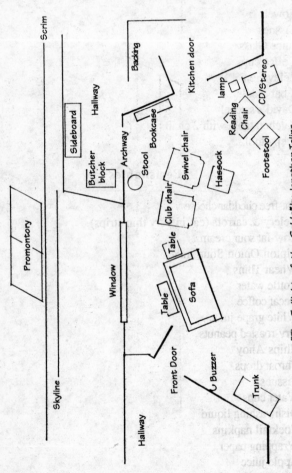

"The Twilight of the Golds" by Jonathan Tolins
Act I scene design by John Iacovelli © 1994

Cyclorama

Scrim

Skyline

Promontory

Hallway

Window

Table

Table

Sofa

Front Door

Buzzer

Trunk

Sideboard

Butcher block

Hallway

Backing

Archway

Stool

Bookcase

Kitchen door

Club chair

Swivel chair

Hassock

Reading Chair

lamp

CD/Stereo

Footstool

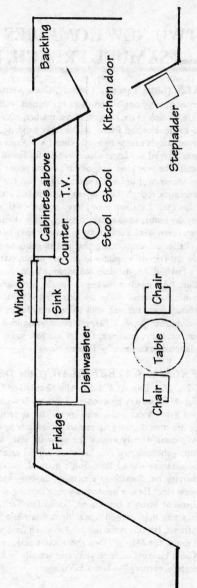

"The Twilight of the Golds" by Jonathan Tolins
Act II scene design by John Iacovelli © 1994

TWO NEW COMEDIES FROM
▬▬▬ SAMUEL FRENCH, Inc.▬▬▬

FAST GIRLS. **(Little Theatre). Comedy.** Diana Amsterdam. 2m., 3f. Int. Lucy Lewis is a contemporary, single woman in her thirties with what used to be called a "healthy sex life," much to the chagrin of her mother, who feels Lucy is too fast, too easy—and too single. Her best friend, on the other hand, neighbor Abigail McBride, is deeply envious of Lucy's ease with men. When Lucy wants to date a man she just calls him up, whereas Abigail sits home alone waiting for Ernest, who may not even know she exists, to call. The only time Abigail isn't by the phone is after Lucy has had a hot date, when she comes over to Lucy's apartment to hear the juicy details and get green with envy. Sometimes, though, Lucy doesn't want to talk about it, which drives Abigail *nuts* ("If you don't tell me about men I have no love life!"). Lucy's mother arrives to take the bull by the horns, so to speak, arriving with a challenge. Mom claims no man will marry Lucy (even were she to *want to* get married), because she's too easy. Lucy takes up the challenge, announcing that she is going to get stalwart ex-boyfriend Sidney ("we're just friends") Epstein to propose to her. Easier said than done. Sidney doesn't *want* a fast girl. Maybe dear old Mom is right, thinks Lucy. Maybe fast girls *can't* have it all. "Amsterdam makes us laugh, listen and think."—Daily Record. "Brilliantly comic moments."—The Monitor. "rapidly paced comedy with a load of laughs . . . a funny entertainment with some pause for reflection on today's [sexual] confusion."—Suburban News. "Takes a penetrating look at [contemporary sexual chaos]. Passion, celibacy, marriage, fidelity are just some of the subjects that Diana Amsterdam hilariously examines."—Tribune News. **(#8149)**

ADVICE FROM A CATERPILLAR. **(Little Theatre.) Comedy.** Douglas Carter Beane. 2m. 2f. 1 Unit set & 1 Int. Ally Sheedy and Dennis Christopher starred in the delightful off-Broadway production of this hip new comedy. Ms. Sheedy played Missy, an avant garde video artist who specializes in re-runs of her family's home videos, adding her own disparaging remarks. Needless to say, she is very alienated from the middle-class, family values she grew up with, which makes her very *au courant*, but strangely unhappy. She has a successful career and a satisfactory love-life with a businessman named Suit. Suit's married, but that doesn't stop him and Missy from carrying on. Something's missing, though—and Missy isn't sure what it is, until she meets Brat. He is a handsome young aspiring actor. Unfortunately, Brat is also the boyfriend of Missy's best friend. Sound familiar? It isn't—because Missy's best friend is a gay man named Spaz! Spaz has been urging Missy to find an unmarried boyfriend, but this is too much—too much for Spaz, too much for Suit and, possibly, too much for Missy. Does she *want* a serious relationship (ugh—how bourgeois!)? Can a bisexual unemployed actor actually be her Mr. Wonderful? "Very funny ... a delightful evening."—Town & Village. **(#3876)**

THE FILM SOCIETY
Jon Robin Baitz
(Little Theatre) Dramatic comedy
4m., 2f. Various ints. (may be unit set)

Imagine the best of Simon Gray crossed with the best of Athol Fugard. The New York critics lavished praise upon this wonderful play, calling Mr. Baitz a major new voice in our theatre. *The Film Society*, set in South Africa, is *not* about the effects of apartheid—at least, overtly. Blenheim is a provincial private school modeled on the second-rate British education machine. It is 1970, a time of complacency for everyone but Terry, a former teacher at Blenheim, who has lost his job because of his connections with Blacks (he invited a Black priest to speak at commencement). Terry tries to involve Jonathan, another teacher at the school and the central character in this play; but Jonathan cares only about his film society, which he wants to keep going at all costs—even if it means programming only safe, non-objectionable, films. When Jonathan's mother, a local rich lady, promises to donate a substantial amount of money to Blenheim if Jonathan is made Headmaster, he must finally choose which side he is on: Terry's or The Establishment's. "Using the school as a microcosm for South Africa, Baitz explores the psychological workings of repression in a society that has to kill its conscience in order to persist in a course of action it knows enough to abhor but cannot afford to relinquish."—New Yorker. "What distinguishes Mr. Baitz' writing, aside from its manifest literacy, is its ability to embrace the ambiguities of political and moral dilemmas that might easily be reduced to blacks and whites."—N.Y. Times. "A beautiful, accomplished play . . . things I thought I was a churl still to value or expect—things like character, plot and theatre dialogue—really do matter."—N.Y. Daily News.   (#8123)

THE SUBSTANCE OF FIRE
Jon Robin Baitz
(Little Theatre.) Drama
3m., 2f. 2 Ints.

Isaac Geldhart, the scion of a family-owned publisher in New York which specializes in scholarly books, suddenly finds himself under siege. His firm is under imminent threat of a corporate takeover, engineered by his own son, Aaron, who watches the bottom line and sees the firm's profitability steadily declining. Aaron wants to publish a trashy novel which will certainly bring in the bucks; whereas Isaac wants to go on publishing worthy scholarly efforts such as his latest project, a multi-volume history of Nazi medical experiments during the Holocaust. Aaron has the bucks to effectively wrench control of the company from his father—or, rather, he has the yen (Japanese businessmen are backing him). What he needs are the votes of the other minority shareholders: his brother Martin and sister Sarah. Like Aaron, they have lived their lives under the thumb of Isaac's imperiousness; and, reluctantly, they agree to side with Aaron against the old man. In the second act, we are back in the library of Isaac's townhouse, a few years later. Isaac has been forcibly retired and has gotten so irascible and eccentric that he may possibly be *non compos mentis*. His children think so, which is why they have asked a psychiatric social worker from the court to interview Isaac to judge his competence. Isaac, who has survived the Holocaust and the death of his wife to build an important publishing company from scratch, must now face his greatest challenge—to persuade Marge Hackett that he is sane. "A deeply compassionate play."—N.Y. Times. "A remarkably intelligent drama. Baitz assimilates and refracts this intellectual history without stinting either on heart or his own original vision."—N.Y. Newsday.   (#21379)

THE NORMAL HEART

(Advanced Groups.) Drama. Larry Kramer. 8m., 1f. Unit set. The New York Shakespeare Festival had quite a success with this searing drama about public and private indifference to the Acquired Immune Deficiency Syndrome plague, commonly called AIDS, and about one man's lonely fight to wake the world up to the crisis. The play has subsequently been produced to great acclaim in London and Los Angeles. Brad Davis originated the role of Ned Weeks, a gay activist enraged at the foot-dragging of both elected public officials and the gay community itself regarding AIDS. Ned not only is trying to save the world from itself, he also must confront the personal toll of AIDS when his lover contracts the disease and ultimately dies. This is more than just a gay play about a gay issue. This is a public health issue which affects all of us. He further uses this theatrical platform to plead with gay brethren to stop thinking of themselves only in terms of their sexuality, and that rampant sexual promiscuity will not only almost guarantee that they will contract AIDS; it is also bad for them as human beings. "An angry, unremitting and gripping piece of political theatre."—N.Y. Daily News. "Like the best social playwright, Kramer produces a cross-fire of life and death energies that illuminate the many issues and create a fierce and moving human drama."—Newsweek. $4.50. (Royalty $60-$40.) Slightly Restricted.   (#788)

A QUIET END

(Adult Groups.) Drama. Robin Swados. 5m. Int. Three men—a schoolteacher, an aspiring jazz pianist and an unemployed actor—have been placed in a run-down Manhattan apartment. All have lost their jobs, all have been shunned by their families, and all have AIDS. They have little in common, it seems, apart from their slowing evolving, albeit uneasy, friendships with each other, and their own mortality. The interaction of the men with a psychiatrist (heard but not seen throughout the course of the play) and the entrance into this arena of the ex-lover of one of the three—seemingly healthy, yet unsure of his future—opens up the play's true concerns: the meaning of friendship, loyalty and love. By celebrating the lives of four men who, in the face of death, become more fearlessly life-embracing instead of choosing the easier path to a quiet end, the play explores the human side of the AIDS crisis, examining how we choose to lead our lives—and how we choose to end them. "The play, as quiet in its message as in its ending, gets the measure of pain and love in a bitter-chill climate."—N.Y. Post. "In a situation that will be recognizable to most gay people, it is the chosen family rather than the biological family, that has become important to these men. Robin Swados has made an impressive debut with A Quiet End by accurately representing the touching relationships in such a group."—N.Y. Native. (Royalty $60-$40.) Music Note: Samuel French, Inc. can supply a cassette tape of music from the original New York production, composed by Robin Swados, upon receipt of a refundable deposit of $25.00, (tape must be returned within one week from the close of your production) and a rental fee of $15.00 per performance. Use of this music in productions is optional.   (#19017)

Other Publications for Your Interest

OTHER PEOPLE'S MONEY
(LITTLE THEATRE—DRAMA)

By JERRY STERNER

3 men, 2 women—One Set

Wall Street takeover artist Lawrence Garfinkle's intrepid computer is going "tilt" over the undervalued stock of New England Wire & Cable. He goes after the vulnerable company, buying up its stock to try and take over the company at the annual meeting. If the stockholders back Garfinkle, they will make a bundle—but what of the 1200 employees? What of the local community? Too bad, says Garfinkle, who would then liquidate the company—take the money and run. Set against the charmingly rapacious financier are Jorgenson, who has run the company since the Year One and his chief operations officer, Coles, who understands, unlike the genial Jorgenson, what a threat Garfinkle poses to the firm. They bring in Kate, a bright young woman lawyer, who specializes in fending off takeovers—and who is the daughter of Jorgenson's administrative assistant, Bea. Kate must not only contend with Garfinkle—she must also move Jorgenson into taking decisive action. Should they use "greenmail"? Try to find a "White Knight"? Employ a "shark repellent"? This compelling drama about Main Street vs. Wall Street is as topical and fresh as today's headlines, giving its audience an inside look at what's *really going on* in this country and asking trenchant questions, not the least of which is whether a corporate raider is really the creature from the Black Lagoon of capitalism or the Ultimate Realist come to save business from itself.

(#17064)

THE DOWNSIDE
(LITTLE THEATRE—COMEDY)

By RICHARD DRESSER

6 men, 2 women—Combination Interior

These days, American business is a prime target for satire, and no recent play has cut as deep, with more hilarious results, than this superb new comedy from the Long Wharf Theatre, Mark & Maxwell, a New Jersey pharmaceuticals firm, has acquired U.S. rights to market an anti-stress drug manufactured in Europe, pending F.D.A. approval; but the marketing executives have got to come up with a snazzy ad campaign by January—and here we are in December! The irony is that nowhere is this drug more needed than right there at Mark & Maxwell, a textbook example of corporate ineptitude, where it seems all you have to do to get ahead is look good in a suit. The marketing strategy meetings get more and more pointless and frenetic as the deadline approaches. These meetings are "chaired" by Dave, the boss, who is never actually there—he is a voice coming out of a box, as Dave phones while jetting to one meeting or another, eventually directing the ad campaign on his mobile phone while his plane is being hijacked! Doesn't matter to Dave, though—what matters is the possible "downside" of this new drug: hallucinations. "Ridiculous", says the senior marketing executive Alan: who then proceeds to tell how Richard Nixon comes to his house in the middle of the night to visit..."Richard Dresser's deft satirical sword pinks the corporate image repeatedly, leaving the audience amused but thoughtful."—Meriden Record. "Funny and ruthlessly cynical."—Phila. Inquirer. "A new comedy that is sheer delight."—Westport News. "The Long Wharf audience laughed a lot, particularly those with office training. But they were also given something to ponder about the way we get things done in America these days, or rather pretend to get things done. No wonder the Japanese are winning."—L.A. Times.

(#6718)

Other Publications for Your Interest

I'M NOT RAPPAPORT
(LITTLE THEATRE—COMEDY)

By HERB GARDNER

5 men, 2 women—Exterior

Just when we thought there would never be another joyous, laugh-filled evening on Broadway, along came this delightful play to restore our faith in the Great White Way. If you thought *A Thousand Clowns* was wonderful, wait til you take a look at *I'm Not Rappaport!* Set in a secluded spot in New York's Central Park, the play is about two octogenarians determined to fight off all attempts to put them out to pasture. Talk about an odd couple! Nat is a lifelong radical determined to fight injustice (real or imagined) who is also something of a spinner of fantasies. He has a delightful repertoire of eccentric personas, which makes the role an actor's dream. The other half of this unlikely partnership is Midge, a Black apartment super who spends his days in the park hiding out from tenants, who want him to retire. "Rambunctiously funny."—N.Y. Post. "A warm and entertaining evening."—W.W. Daily. **Tony Award Winner, Best Play 1986. Posters.**

(#11071)

(Royalty, $60-$40.)

CROSSING DELANCEY
(LITTLE THEATRE—COMEDY)

By SUSAN SANDLER

2 men, 3 women—Comb. Interior/Exterior.

Isabel is a young Jewish woman who lives alone and works in a NYC bookshop. When she is not pining after a handsome author who is one of her best customers, she is visiting her grandmother—who lives by herself in the "old neighborhood", Manhattan's Lower East Side. Isabel is in no hurry to get married, which worries her grandmother. The delightfully nosey old lady hires an old friend who is—can you believe this in the 1980's?—a matchmaker. Bubbie and the matchmaker come up with a Good Catch for their Isabel—Sam, a young pickle vendor. Sam is no *schlemiel*, though. He likes Isabel; but he knows he is going to have to woo her, which he proceeds to do. When Isabel realizes what a cad the author is, and what a really nice man Sam is, she begins to respond; and the end of the play is really a beginning, ripe with possibilities for Isabel and "An amusing interlude for theatregoers who may have thought that simple romance and sentimentality had long since been relegated to television sitcoms...tells its unpretentious story believeably, rarely trying to make its gag lines, of which there are many, upstage its narration or outshine its heart."—N.Y. Times. "A warm and loving drama...a welcome addition to the growing body of Jewish dramatic work in this country."—Jewish Post and Opinion.

(#5739)

(Royalty, $50-$40.)
